ON FOREIGN SOIL

ON FOREIGN SOIL

*To Janet,
With warmest wishes to a dear friend and fellow Forester. Best always,
Jerome F. Ryan
6-19-04*

Jerome F. Ryan

Copyright © 2004 by Jerome F. Ryan

All rights reserved. No part of this book shall be reproduced or transmitted in any form or by any means, electronic, mechanical, magnetic, photographic including photocopying, recording or by any information storage and retrieval system, without prior written permission of the publisher. No patent liability is assumed with respect to the use of the information contained herein. Although every precaution has been taken in the preparation of this book, the publisher and author assume no responsibility for errors or omissions. Neither is any liability assumed for damages resulting from the use of the information contained herein.

This is a work of fiction. Names, characters, places, and incidents either are the product of the author's imagination or are used fictitiously. Any resemblance to actual events or locales or persons, living or dead, is entirely coincidental.

ISBN 0-7414-1947-5

Published by:

519 West Lancaster Avenue
Haverford, PA 19041-1413
Info@buybooksontheweb.com
www.buybooksontheweb.com
Toll-free (877) BUY BOOK
Local Phone (610) 520-2500
Fax (610) 519-0261

Printed in the United States of America

Printed on Recycled Paper

Published March 2004

Dedication

This book is dedicated to my parents, Earl Edward Ryan (deceased) and Vivian Gray Ryan.

To Dad, for his encouragement and help, which he had freely given whether for school work or for scouting. He was always there, to lend support or provide example. Somehow, I know that he is still there, guiding me along, inspiring me to reach for the stars.

To Mom, who, through her life-long example, showed her family a world of richness lying between the book covers. Whether it is for entertainment or learning, she was never without a book nearby.

Even in early childhood, she treasured her library card, as the key that opened the doors to a wealth of knowledge and triggered her imagination. She was a constant visitor to the library, and certainly must have read every volume on the shelves.

Mom and Dad, I dedicate this book to you.

Acknowledgements

I wish to acknowledge, and thank, my sister, Mrs. Sheila Ryan Wallace, a writer and published author, who has willingly shared her love and enthusiasm for writing with me. Her invaluable advice and suggestions led to the publication of this book.

Appreciation is also extended to Mrs. Elinor Curtin Cameron, who freely and willingly assisted in the editing process, both in language usage and grammatical punctuation. Her extensive wealth of literary knowledge, and her generous concern, has greatly aided in making this book a reality.

Many thanks also go to friends and family, who have encouraged me to draw upon my earlier travels for others to enjoy. They have been an inspiration, as I learned to blend the reality of former experiences with the fiction of imagination. For these are truly the essential keys to an interesting and entertaining novel.

Contents

Chapter 1	Good News	1
Chapter 2	Departure Day	9
Chapter 3	Danish Dilemma	18
Chapter 4	Moscow Arrival	28
Chapter 5	The Kremlin	40
Chapter 6	Suspicious Activity	53
Chapter 7	The Circus	69
Chapter 8	The Rendezvous	79
Chapter 9	The Army Camp	92
Chapter 10	Zwenigorod and Khubinkah	103
Chapter 11	Gumshoes	114
Chapter 12	The Exchange	127
Chapter 13	The Warehouse	138
Chapter 14	Fancy Footwork	149
Chapter 15	The Commissioner	158
Epilogue	Unexpected Visitor	166

Chapter One

Good News

The front door shut with a thud as mom walked into the kitchen. I had just finished breakfast and was about to leave for the library to do some research for a history assignment.

"Jimmy, this is for you. I think it's what you've been waiting for," my mother said, while sliding a letter across the table.

The large brown envelope had arrived just moments earlier, which was unusual for a Saturday morning. The letter carrier had never come before noon on Saturdays. It was the letter from the Teen Ambassador Program (TAP) that I had been expecting. They had said that they would send me a decision about the interview I had had with them earlier in December. I hesitated a moment, hoping that I had been accepted. I almost didn't want to open it, fearing the worse.

"Well, aren't you going to open it?" my mother asked impatiently.

I knew that she was just as excited as I was, maybe even more. I tore it open and nervously fumbled with the folded letter as the envelope fell to the floor. I read it twice while the news slowly registered in my head.

"Mom, I can't believe it. I've been accepted," I yelled, while holding the letter out for her to read.

"I knew it. I just knew it, Jimmy. Let me see," she said.

With obvious excitement, she read it aloud while emphasizing each important line.

"Jimmy, this is great. You have the chance of a lifetime. Wait till your father hears the news."

I had actually been accepted to serve as a Teen Ambassador. I didn't think I had done well on the interviews, but apparently I had. Mom was perhaps even more excited than I was.

"Wow," she exclaimed. "I knew you would be accepted. I just knew it," she repeated, while running to the phone to spread the news to all her friends and even to neighbors, too.

Actually, I knew nothing about being a teenage ambassador or what would be expected from me, but I hoped to find the answers at the orientation meetings planned for the Spring.

Word of my acceptance had spread like wildfire throughout the town, and soon even the local newspaper wanted to write an article about my selection. I learned that another girl from my high school, Erin Parker, had also been selected. I didn't know her, but was sure that we would meet at some point. I decided that 1994 was going to be a year to remember.

Monthly orientation meetings were conducted by our Delegation Leader, Mr. Reilly, a stern man who didn't smile much. Many students thought he would be very strict and resigned themselves to just follow his rules. He had his funny side too, and would often fumble through some papers that he had removed from his black briefcase. He always carried that briefcase with him. It was filled with students' paperwork, a small First Aid kit, medicines, and a large half-filled bottle of some pink liquid. He was always complaining about an upset stomach and sometimes disappeared with that pink bottle. He returned later and put the bottle back into his briefcase, after giving the cap an extra twist. He said that it was for the students' use, but we knew that it was really for him.

Mr. Reilly was a seasoned traveler, and had the final say on the students chosen to participate each year in the Teen Ambassador Program summer travels. He told the students that our goal was to promote goodwill overseas. Only above-average students had been selected to travel as young representatives, sharing their culture and friendship with those they met.

Pretty easy, I had thought, so I applied. I was very surprised and fortunate to be chosen for this high honor and looked forward to a summer adventure overseas.

During the spring orientation meetings, we received detailed instruction on local history, culture, and etiquette to help prepare our delegation for summer travel. Mr. Reilly said he wanted us to get to know each other and become 'a family,' as he called us. This is why he planned group activities and ice breakers at each meeting. This year we were going to visit Moscow. My parents and I were really excited when he announced the itinerary and described famous landmarks that we would see and visit.

At our first formal meeting in January, Mr. Reilly introduced his two assistants, Mrs. Kolinsky and Mrs. Renaud. Like him, they were also teachers and this was their first trip overseas with students. All three leaders were well liked, and we knew that we could go to them with any problems that we had.

The two women became good friends during the TAP meetings as they shared a common interest in both school things and travel. It seemed as though Mrs. Kolinsky had traveled extensively and studied about many countries. Mrs. Renaud, on the other hand, had not traveled before, except within the United States. Her husband was afraid of airplanes, she said. This kept her from any long distance travel. He finally passed away last year. I think she said it was some kind of cancer. Both women were very nice, and often sat and told us stories about what things were like when they were growing up.

Mrs. Kolinsky said that she had been born in Poland in 1945. She told us about the Russians requiring everyone learn their language in school. Eventually, her parents had fled to the United States in 1960. She said that she was only fifteen years old, and had struggled to learn English while attending public school. Her parents had found work in one of the shoe shops in Haverhill, Massachusetts. I think she said Ballen Shoe Products. She said that they went out of business in the 70's, as more and more manufacturing moved to the South where labor was cheaper.

Both Mrs. Kolinsky and Mrs. Renaud have taught nearly all subjects in elementary schools for many years. They both showed a real interest in the kids in our group and were a big help to Mr. Reilly.

As for Mr. Reilly, well, he was always a mystery. He seldom had spoken about himself and remained rather aloof. The students never knew if he was pleasant or just a mean old man who found little enjoyment in life. He certainly was well organized, however, and quite a capable and efficient Delegation Leader but still somewhat of an enigma.

Often I would arrive at the orientation meetings just after they started. They were held in the old wooden-framed Brookville Town Hall. My dad worked late, so we would usually scurry up the steps and into the large assembly room on the second floor where we always found empty seats in the back. Mom was the note taker while dad and I just sat and listened.

The large austere room had eight foot high windows with shades neatly aligned half way. Photographs of all the ex-mayors seemingly dating back to Napoleon, adorned the spaces between the windows. At the front of the room was a small stage with an old American flag standing alone on the left side. In front of the stage was a single table where Mr. Reilly stood. It was filled with papers and handouts. Altogether, there were thirty-seven student ambassadors, although there were often other kids at the meetings, sitting with their parents and listening. They might have been younger brothers or sisters, I imagined.

Glancing around, I tried, unsuccessfully, to see if there were anyone I knew. Suddenly my searching stopped. My eyes focused on a young girl just a few rows ahead of me. She was a very attractive girl with long auburn hair. Sitting attentively with her parents, she took notes about each topic. I couldn't seem to take my eyes off her. I certainly wanted to meet her but we seldom made eye contact. She left quickly at the end of the meetings. I didn't think she would ever notice me. At each meeting I would seek her out and look for an opportunity to meet her. In March, my luck changed. I was paired with her in an ice breaker activity. She had an enticing smile, soft gentle features, and blue eyes. She wore a plaid skirt and an angora sweater with the sleeves pushed up above her elbows. Her hair was pulled back and tied into a pony tail that fell just below her shoulders. She had a well-developed figure, and appeared to be slightly shorter than I was.

Before the ice breaker started, I hurriedly introduced myself while still trying to act cool.

"Hi, I'm Jimmy Reynolds, and you are?"

"Hi. I'm Erin Parker."

"What? No way," I replied. "I don't believe it. This is really strange."

So this is the girl who goes to my high school, I thought.

"Why are you acting so strange?" she asked with a puzzled look.

"Gee, we both go to the same high school, and yet I've never met you. Heck, I've never even seen you. I did see your name, though, in the newspaper story they wrote about the Teen Ambassador Program," I continued, "but I never put a face with the name. I'm a senior and you're a junior. Right?"

"Yuh, I'm in Mrs. Grady's homeroom over in the J Wing."

"J Wing, huh? That's on the other side of the school from me. I'm in the S Wing. That doesn't give us much of a chance to meet. You know we have different schedules and all," I continued.

"Yuh, I know. I'm really excited about this trip, aren't you?"

"Uh-huh, but I didn't think I'd be accepted."

"Me too. Say, why did you sign up for this trip anyway?" Erin inquired.

"Oh, I love traveling and this seemed like a great opportunity to see some of the world that I wouldn't otherwise see. Imagine, we're really going to Russia. After I graduate, I'll be tied up with college, and who knows what will happen then. Actually, I didn't think I'd be accepted, and I thought that I really bombed the interview, but here I am."

"I know what you mean. I didn't think I'd be selected either, but I wanted to try anyway. I guess we will be traveling together this summer after all." she continued.

"I guess we will," I replied. "Maybe we can get together after school sometime and talk more about the trip."

"Sounds okay to me. Oh, we'd better get back to this activity. Mr. Reilly is coming."

We never did find seats together at the other monthly meetings and only met at school a couple times, but we did agree to sit together on the plane and chat some more. She was an interesting girl, and I was becoming quite interested of her.

Chapter Two

Departure Day

July fourteenth, our long-awaited departure day, finally arrived. Joey, my kid brother, tried unsuccessfully to slowly raise the window shade when suddenly it snapped out of his hand. The shade flew upward and spun around with a loud cracking sound that jolted me awake. The sun flooded my bedroom with a blinding brilliance. I squinted while holding one hand over my eyes.

"What the heck are you doing, Joey? Pull that darn thing down," I demanded. "I'm trying to sleep, you know."

"I know, but mom wanted me to wake you up. She says that you'd better get ready since we're leaving for the airport pretty soon," Joey replied.

"What time is it anyway?"

"Nine fifteen," he said, as he headed into the hallway pulling the door closed behind him.

"Pull the shade back down before you go," I yelled.

"Can't. Too high," he replied, as the door slammed shut behind him.

I had tossed and turned all night, before eventually falling asleep. Still exhausted, I yanked the blankets over my head, in a vain attempt to hide from the glaring sunlight. It was useless.

Today I would travel with the student delegation to Russia. I had waited a long time for this day, and it was now just hours away. Finally I threw the blankets aside, jumped out of bed, and slid into my robe as I headed for my morning shower.

"That you, Jimmy?" my mother called out from the kitchen, as I shuffled toward the bathroom, still half asleep.

"Yuh. I'm going to take a shower."

"Don't forget to pack your toiletries when you're done in there. Your breakfast is almost ready. I'll put it on the table, so don't take too long or it'll be cold," she reminded me.

"Okay, okay. I won't forget."

I took a quick shower, gathered my toilet items, and shoved them into my small shaving kit, before returning to my room to get dressed. My suitcase lay open on the floor across from my bed. I had already packed everything that Mr. Reilly suggested. I then rearranged some items of clothing and squeezed my shaving kit in before zipping it closed. At last, I was ready for travel.

I sat on the edge of my bed staring at the suitcase a long time and thinking of Erin. She was probably already up and going over many last minute details, just as I was. I was quite excited about traveling, and maybe even more about seeing Erin again and spending some quality time getting to know her better. I hoped that we could find two seats together on the plane and not be separated. Mr. Reilly said that we could sit with our friends if we wanted. My main concern was in finding two seats together. I enjoyed talking with Erin and looked forward to sharing this new adventure with her.

After breakfast, dad packed my suitcase in the car, backed out of the driveway, then headed for the airport. Mom was so worried that I might have forgotten to pack various items that she ran through a long checklist of things to assure herself that I was completely prepared.

Luckily there was only moderate traffic as we headed down I-93 and through the Sumner Tunnel to Logan Airport. We discussed again the sights and places that we'd see, and, of course, dad gave his customary sermon with words of caution about matters of security. I knew that they'd worry about me, but they would have to deal with it. They also were aware that I was very responsible and could handle myself properly.

We assembled at the Trans-Atlantic check-in counter where Mr. Reilly was waiting. He welcomed me, then grabbed my luggage and swung it onto the scales. He handed the airline representative my ticket and passport. After checking in, the agent handed me a boarding pass, and I was now free to roam about until departure time.

Across the concourse, I saw Erin enter the terminal and give her bag to Mr. Reilly. Her parents chatted with him for a few moments while Erin searched about. I waved to her, and she eventually spotted me and waved back with a broad smile.

She was dressed rather chic with tailored khaki slacks and an open collared blue shirt. A red neckerchief trimmed her neckline. A light jacket was thrown over her arms, and her reddish-brown hair was tied back on a pony tail. She said something to her parents and then headed my way.

"Hi, Erin. Right on time, I see. This is really exciting. I can't believe that today actually arrived. It won't be long till we're on our way," I said.

"I know. Imagine, six months of preparation and our adventure is finally starting."

She then untied her long reddish-brown hair, allowing it to cascade gently down over her soft shoulders and framing her delicate face. She said that her hair was too bothersome to keep up and she preferred to let it fall naturally.

"How was your ride in?" I asked.

"Okay. We would have been here sooner except that my father was held up awhile due to a bad accident in Reading. Somebody jumped a red light and ran into another car. At least, that's what it looked like. Oh, there's Carol and Maureen. I've gotta see them for a minute. Wait here, Jimmy, I'll be right back," she added as she turned and worked her way through the crowded terminal.

She stopped briefly, turned, and gave me a half wave and warm smile before disappearing into the crowd. I smiled back instinctively even though she had already turned away.

Mr. Reilly was still busy checking-in other students. His two assistant delegation leaders finally arrived and helped him complete the in-processing. Once satisfied that everyone was present, Mr. Reilly called for a brief meeting in an open area nearby. Basically, it was a short reassurance session for the parents' benefit. He then directed us toward our departure gate. Handshakes, kisses, and hugs preceded tear-filled good-byes. Off we bravely went, down the long airport corridors to our waiting plane.

The Flight Attendants directed our whole delegation to a block of seats in the rear of the plane, while our leaders sat together ahead of us. Erin and I quickly claimed two empty seats by a window.

Before long, the plane taxied onto the runway, and, with engines roaring, raced forward, gained speed, and slowly lifting upward. The students let out a loud cheer as our journey began in earnest. The long overseas flight was smooth and uneventful and the enthusiasm of earlier gave way to quiet moments and soft conversations. Erin and I chatted nearly non-stop about anything that came to mind.

"Did you see Mr. Reilly back there at the airport, Erin? He was like a robot grabbing everyone's suitcases and twirling around and throwing them onto the scales with one hand and handing the agent the student's ticket with the other," I laughed.

"I must have missed it when I went over to see Carol and Maureen. I bet he was funny. I was curious about Carol's interview three weeks ago at Stevens University. She went there in June, just for the experience, and to see how she might do next year when she has to select some college and do it for real. She'll be a senior then, like you, and she'll have to really do well in order to get in. She says that her grades aren't the best, and that makes it tough for her."

"What did she say about the interview?" I asked Erin. "Was she nervous? Say, doesn't Carol go to school over in Pleasant Grove? I think I've seen her at Walker when we played football against them last Fall."

"Uh huh, she's a cheerleader at Walker High and loves it. A great kid, but overly worried about college."

"That's it. I knew that I knew her from somewhere. Too bad, they beat us. They had a really awesome team that chewed us apart in the first half. Well, anyway, how was her interview at Stevens University?" I again asked.

Our conversations weaved back and forth as we turned our attention from Carol to other kids in our group and to those we knew back at school. We also recalled and laughed about some of the funny ice breakers that we had participated in during the Spring orientation meetings.

A few hours later the flight attendant announced that we were approaching Stockholm. During our two hour layover in the Swedish capital, we enjoyed more free time. We were allowed to wander, but not far from our new departure point, Gate 17A. Erin and I strolled along the concourse commenting on various merchandise in the store windows along the way.

"Hey, look at these, Jimmy," she said, while stopping at a newsstand."

"Look at what?" I asked.

"The newspapers. Look at how many they have and all the strange languages they are printed in."

"Yuh, I saw a newspaper place in Boston that had lots of foreign papers too, just like this one." I replied.

"Here's one in English. It must be from England, I think. No, it's the Cleveland Chronicle," she laughed as she returned the paper to its slot.

After skimming some of the headlines, we drifted further along the concourse to a small coffee shop with a few empty tables and chairs. We draped our day-bags and jackets over the backs of the chairs. Erin then collapsed, slouching down in her chair, while I skimmed the suspended menu behind the counter.

"Want some coffee?" I asked Erin.

"Sounds good to me," she said, as I headed to the counter.

"Cream and one sugar, please," she added while straightening herself in the chair.

I bought two cups of coffee and raced back to the table as quickly as I could. The coffee was very hot and my hands were burning from the cardboard cups.

"Ouch. This is really hot. Be careful," I advised Erin, while blowing on my fingers.

"Thanks Jimmy. Did you burn your hands?" she asked.

"No. But, boy, were they ever hot," I said while still fanning my hands in the air.

With fresh coffee in hand, we slowly sipped and chatted some more. I could see that Erin was tired but still filled with expectation and excitement. She always had something to say and showed a sincere and concerned interest in whatever we talked about. She had a bubbly, outgoing personality and was a good conversationalist too. She always seemed to find nice things to say about people.

My feelings for Erin had been growing stronger ever since I met her back in January, but I was not sure about her feelings toward me. Some times she seemed to like me, and other times I just wasn't sure. Call it a gut feeling if you wish. In any event, I knew that I would know better how she felt by the end of this trip.

I sat back, took a long sip of coffee and thought back to those quiet moments on the plane. I had been content just sitting close to her, feeling the warmth and softness of her body next to mine as I thought about the days ahead.

Chapter Three

Danish Dilemma

Mrs. Kolinsky roamed the concourse in search of students meandering about. She spoke briefly with each student she met, directing him or her to the departure gate. Eventually, she arrived at the coffee kiosk, stopping at our table.

"Hi Erin, Jimmy. Having a good time so far?" she asked.

"Yuh. Can't wait till we actually get to Moscow," I replied.

"Oh, be patient. We'll be there early this evening. That is, if our connecting flight isn't delayed or cancelled."

"Is it still scheduled to leave on time?" Erin asked.

"Yes. I think so. Say, you'd better hurry up with your coffee, Erin. Mr. Reilly has something important he wants to tell everyone. We're all going to meet in the departure lounge for a short meeting. Better come along and don't forget your jacket,

Jimmy," she said, while pointing toward the floor behind my chair.

Looking around, I saw that my jacket had slipped off the back of my chair and now lay in a neat clump on the floor.

"Oh thanks, Mrs. Kolinsky," I replied as I reached down to retrieve it. "What's the meeting about?"

"I don't know. He's been talking with some young man he met a little while ago. I think he wants to introduce him or something, but I'm not sure. Get your things and come along," she continued.

"Are you finished with that coffee, Erin?" I asked, while brushing off my jacket.

She had been nursing her coffee for nearly half an hour and must surely be finished, I thought. I wanted to hurry her along so that we could see what Mr. Reilly wanted and find out what that young guy was about.

"I'm ready when you are, Jimmy," Erin said, as she took one last gulp of the coffee that had long since turned cold.

Erin gathered her things and I disposed of our trash in a large trash receptacle next to the serving counter. Grabbing my jacket, I urged Erin to hurry along.

"We'd better get going, Erin. I can see that Mr. Reilly has that new guy with him and everyone is already there. He must be the one Mrs. Kolinsky told us about," I said, as I hurried down the concourse, still sliding my arms into my jacket sleeves.

Erin swung her sweater behind her back and tied its sleeves loosely around her neck. She then tossed her day-bag over her shoulders and hurried along with me. We wasted no time heading toward the waiting group of students at the far end of the concourse. Most were already seated on the polished floor in front of the large terminal windows. We hurried to an open area at the back of the departure lounge. There was very little free space left on the marble floor when we arrived.

"Quick, Erin. There is an open spot down in the back."

We carefully stepped over and around the seated students toward the last remaining free space. We were next to a vending machine and squeezed in, with barely enough room to cross our legs.

Mr. Reilly signaled Mrs. Renaud to begin her headcount. She pointed to each student as she called out a number. Once satisfied that we were all present, she informed Mr. Reilly who was still talking with the young man, and pointing to some papers in his hand. He spoke in a very low whisper, and then turned to the waiting students.

The young man was slightly less than six feet and had a rugged build. His medium brown hair fell just below his shirt collar. As he waited, he rolled up the sleeves of his dark maroon shirt and tugged at his dark tight-fitting jeans.

After a few minutes, Mr. Reilly raised his hand as a sign for the students to give him their attention. A hush spread across our group as the young man slowly stepped away and leaned against a deserted check-in booth. All eyes were now focused on Mr. Reilly as he began to speak.

"May I have your attention, please? A short while ago I called the TAP office back home to confirm our safe arrival. They were pleased, as I knew they would be. Then they advised me that a new student would join our group here in Stockholm. They said that he'd meet us at the plane before we made our final connecting flight to Moscow," he explained.

"No sooner did I hang up the phone when I learned that this young man was seeking me out. His name is Billy Martin. His folks work at the American Consulate in Denmark, and I hope you will welcome him into our delegation. He has been studying the orientation materials that you all received at the meetings, and now he wants to travel to Moscow," Mr. Reilly continued.

He then turned to Billy and motioned for him to step forward.

"Billy, would you like to say a few words?"

Billy straightened up, tucked his shirt snugly under his belt, and stepped forward to where Mr. Reilly was standing. He seemed somewhat nervous as he spoke in a quiet tone, barely audible in the rear of the lounge.

"Hi. My name Billy Martin. I live in Lystrup, Denmark and look forward to traveling with you. I study from da books that da TAP people send me. I speak Danish and not so good English. I speak some Russian too. My father is a diplomat so I live many places and learn languages. I study much about Russia and want to see it. I am happy to meet you," he said, while gesturing with a short wave.

"Welcome Billy. From now on you're one of us. Guess that's it for now, gang," Mr. Reilly said. Pausing a moment, he added "Oh yes, Mrs. Renaud has landing cards that each of you must take and complete before we land in Moscow. They'll be collected by the Customs people there. Don't forget to fill it out and don't lose it," Mr. Reilly cautioned.

"Gee, this is a real surprise. What do you think of this guy, Jimmy?" Erin asked.

"I don't know. I don't know why they didn't tell us sooner," I replied. "Seems strange for him to just pop out of nowhere."

"He sure is a hunk, don't you think?" Erin observed.

"Oh, spare me the heart throb," I said while giving her a slight push.

We both laughed as we climbed to our feet and gathered our belongings.

Mrs. Renaud had already started to distribute the landing cards to everyone before they scattered. She handed one to Erin and to me. After skimming it over, I put it in my back-pack for safe keeping. Some students were already gathering around Billy to welcome him to our group.

"What do you say, Erin? Want to go over and say hi?"

"Of course, silly."

Most of the students had already gone to welcome Billy. Wasting no time, Erin had already started heading toward him too, while I tagged along. I could hear Billy trying to explain where his home town, Lystrup, was.

"Yuh, it ist in Jutland. Dis da land on west side of Denmark. Very cool and raw. Not too good for da health," he continued.

Finally, Erin and I nudged our way closer and shook hands with Billy as we welcomed him. He was polite and smiled a lot. He seemed like a regular guy and might fit in with our group nicely, I thought.

"What did you study in Denmark?" I asked Billy.

"Oh, I take many subjects, but I like da languages most. I vont to learn English more better," he replied.

At this point, Erin, who had been sizing him up, added "Well, if you want to learn some English, maybe I can help. I'm real good with English in school."

Billy smiled at Erin. His eyes seemed fixed on her a long time. Erin returned his smile and seemed to blush, as he continued smiling at her.

"Yes, thank you. I like maybe to do that," he finally responded.

At this point I willingly made room for other students to welcome Billy to our delegation. We told him that we'd see him later and then stepped aside.

"What was that all about, Erin? Oh, I can help you learn English better," I said mockingly. "I bet he knows more English than he's lettin' on," I added. "And did you see the way he was looking at you?"

"Oh, so look who's jealous now."

"What? Me? I'm not jealous," I replied.

"What? Okay, Jimmy, and just who do you think you're kidding anyway? You are so transparent," Erin continued.

"Okay. Okay. So I'm concerned that he might take you up on your offer and I won't see you much," I confessed.

"Relax, Jimmy, you don't need as much help as he does. But there are times when I don't understand you at all," she added with a sheepish and perplexed grin.

Loud speakers overhead echoed throughout the concourse, announcing that our flight was boarding at Gate 42. This was an unexpected gate change, and we quickly grabbed our things and headed down the long concourse like a mob without direction. We spread out from side to side much to the consternation of travelers heading in the opposite direction. Mrs. Kolinsky tried her best to usher our group to the right side of the concourse but with little success. Soon we arrived at Gate 42.

I could see that Billy had become an instant hit as a small group of admiring girls clustered about him asking him many questions. This was fine with me for I was content to enjoy these added moments of privacy with Erin without worrying about him.

Passengers, with tickets in hand, were already starting through the gate.

"Passports, please," the stewardess called out in a loud voice.

The large group of travelers slowly proceeded toward the gate, with their tickets and passports in hand. Some dragged their carry-on luggage while others simply hand-carried small bundles. The impatient crowd pressed forward toward the uniformed SAS airline stewardess who carefully screened each passenger.

Erin and I held out our tickets and passports and waited while the stewardess scanned the tickets through her computer. She then opened our passports and skimmed through them, checking that everything was as it should be. Apparently satisfied that our documents were in order, she allowed us to pass through.

The large plane was only half full. Most passengers had claimed seats in the forward and middle sections. Our seats, however, were in the rear. We squeezed down the long narrow aisles with our carry-on baggage and jackets in tow. Our three Delegation Leaders sat on the opposite side. I unzipped my back-pack and pulled the landing card that Mrs. Renaud had given to me earlier. After filling out the card I handed my pen to Erin. We knew that we would need these cards upon arrival in Moscow. Erin quickly completed her card and then sat back and waited for take-off.

After a short while, our plane slowly backed away from the jet-way and started to maneuver towards the distant runway. With roaring engines, we again raced along a wide runway and climbed upward into the early evening haze.

"Next stop, Moscow," Erin exclaimed, with much enthusiasm. "In a few more hours we'll be there."

"You're really hyped up about Moscow, I see. You know that it'll be really dark when we arrive, so don't count on seeing much," I cautioned.

"I know, but I'll see enough on our way to the hotel. Aren't you excited, Jimmy?"

"Oh, yuh, of course I am."

Working their way toward us, down the long, narrow aisle, two flight attendants served light meals and beverages.

"Look, Erin," I said, pointing up the aisle. "We've got another meal coming."

"Oh, no. I'm stuffed. Think I'll pass this time. You can have mine," she said.

After the meal, the cabin lights dimmed, and she leaned back and closed her eyes.

Chapter Four

Moscow Arrival

Our long journey was finally drawing to a close. We had flown nearly non-stop from Boston with just one layover in Stockholm and were now approaching Moscow. The monotonous flights had taken their toll on the once-excited students in our group. At last, we began our long descent to the Moscow International Airport. Erin and I had talked mostly about the new boy, Billy, and about Russian sights during the relatively short flight from Stockholm. She said that she loved to travel and see things that she had only read about in books. She added that this trip was certainly the most adventurous trip of all.

"Just think, Jimmy," she said, "How many people ever get a chance to visit Russia?"

I had a feeling that this summer's adventure would certainly turn out to be a unique experience for both of us. Erin was really excited about seeing some of the Russian capital. After the in-flight meal she had laid her head on my shoulder and had fallen asleep. I put my head back and closed my eyes while enjoying the scent of her perfume and warmth of her body so close to mine.

Faint chimes signaled that the captain had illuminated the "Fasten Seatbelt" warning. A petite stewardess soon worked her way up the narrow aisle and dutifully checked each passenger's lap belt.

Another announced over the intercom "Ladies and gentlemen, we are starting our approach to the Moscow area. Please make sure that all seat belts are securely fastened, and all seats and trays returned to their upright position."

I knew it was time to wake Erin. I did not want to wake her, as I was quite content to feel her soft body so close to mine. Clutching a small blanket around her neck, she snuggled up to my arm. Her long curly hair partially concealed her tightly closed eyes.

I gently nudged Erin. The blanket slipped from her grasp, as she stretched her arms.

"Come on, Erin, time to wake up," I whispered quietly.

Erin sat up and, with a huge yawn, glanced out the window.

"Are we there yet?" she asked, while rubbing the sleep out of her eyes.

"Almost," I said. "Boy, you sure slept a long time."

"I guess I didn't realize just how tired I was," she replied. "I can't wait to get to the hotel and out of these grungy clothes. I feel like I've been in them for days."

"Oh, come on, it's only been a few hours since we left Boston," I said.

"Yuh, I know, but it seems a lot longer. I like clean clothes. It makes me feel better, so I can enjoy what I'm doing more," she added.

"Oh, I guess I feel the same, but I'm too keyed up to think about hotels right now. The Kremlin, yes; hotels, no. Think we'll pass the Kremlin on our way to the hotel?" I asked.

"I don't know. Maybe. Why are you so hyped up about the Kremlin, Jimmy?"

"Oh, I read a lot about it in school, that it was the seat of the Supreme Soviet and Lenin's Tomb. I'm sort of a history buff," I continued.

"Not me. I came to see how the people live and maybe to get away from home for awhile. They were driving me crazy," she added.

I was puzzled by her comment. I didn't want to pry, yet was curious. Finally, I decided to ask what she meant by it.

"What do you mean? How do they drive you crazy?"

"Oh, my folks have been on my case about school grades and college choices a lot. They keep harping that good grades are the keys to college.

They think I'll learn somethin' about the world by going on this trip. "You socialize too much. Always on the phone," they'd say. Maybe they're right, but I do have a life you know. After all, I am seventeen."

I liked Erin and hoped I could help her change her outlook. I felt that if she could put her folks out of her mind, she'd have a better time. I was feeling even closer to Erin now that we were able to share some inner concerns. Revealing some of her problems convinced me that she was beginning to trust me .

Soon the wheels screeched onto the long runway and the jet engines were thrown into reverse thrust. A loud roar vibrated throughout the plane as it slowed to a crawl before turning onto a taxiway. Erin's attention was quickly drawn to the window taking in all that we passed until we finally arrived at our gate.

After claiming our luggage, we headed towards the Customs Inspection station. A student, waiting in the line next to me, appeared very nervous, as he fumbled with his passport and landing card. I didn't pay much attention to him, as nearly everyone in our delegation was tired and nervous. The line moved slowly. Eventually, it was my turn. I approached the dark uniformed inspector who sat expressionless behind a glass enclosure. His stern appearance would make the bravest of our group tremble with fear. He took my landing card and, after giving a passing glance at my passport, he simply stamped it with a thud and waved me on.

I breathed a sigh of relief, and scrambled across the marble-tiled concourse to join the students gathering outside. Mr. Reilly spoke briefly to our Russian bus driver, and then directed us to our blue and white motor coach. The word 'Sputnik,' was emblazoned in large blue letters on its sides. This bus would be our main transportation for the next seven days, I learned.

Erin had cleared Customs before me and was already at the bus. When I arrived, I saw her struggling to lift her heavy canvas suitcase into the storage area under the bus.

"Here. Let me help," I said.

I also struggled as I attempted to lift her suitcase into the cargo area. After some effort I eventually succeeded. Straightening up, I turned to Erin, wiped my brow, and slowly shook my head.

"Boy, you sure got enough stuff in these bags to last a month."

"Oh, Jimmy, you know that girls need to pack more than boys," she replied.

Trying to act cute, I responded "You didn't forget the family dog, did you?"

She smiled, while slapping me on the arm.

"Why? Did you hear him barking?"

She had a good sense of humor and we laughed as we climbed aboard the idling bus.

"Hey, I see two seats over there," she said, pointing down the aisle.

"Do you want the window seat?" she asked.

"No, it's okay. You go ahead."

We crammed our shoulder bags into the overhead rack and flopped into our seats. A few other students were still trying to negotiate down the narrow aisles as we sat back. We were both tired, and yet, wanted to stay awake to see some of the city. Jet lag and our lack of rest, however, soon overcame any resistance we had to sleep as some students slowly dozed off. Our three chaperones sat in the front, apparently discussing the itinerary and students' sleeping arrangements with the in-country guide, Serge Rachmananov, whom they had met inside the terminal.

The bus slowly pulled away, as Mr. Reilly introduced Serge. In broken English, Serge tried his best to describe the activities and sights that were planned for the following days. The students who were still awake seemed quite attentive yet were actually nearly asleep themselves.

From the airport, we cruised down a crowded four-lane divided highway dodging careless drivers hurrying along. Our driver periodically expressed his displeasure with these thoughtless motorists in the busy late evening traffic by sounding his horn and mumbling something to himself in Russian.

Our journey took us past row upon row of tall four and five story white-bricked apartment complexes. We saw that the grassy areas separating these buildings were not well maintained. Their upkeep was obviously much neglected. The grass had grown at least two feet high except where paths had been beaten down by constant foot traffic. Playground areas near these buildings were markedly bare, most likely where children scuffed their feet as they played. I gazed up at these many buildings, noting that each apartment had a small balcony filled with boxes of stored materials. Little space remained, unfortunately, for residents to enjoy an evening breeze, I thought. Wide, dirt sidewalks lined the main roadways. Puddles gave witness to earlier showers, leaving the walking areas quite slippery. I saw two women pushing their baby carriages along the side of the busy street in spite of the traffic. The congested roadway apparently provided a more desirable alternative to the deplorable sidewalks.

Soon we arrived at the Hotel Metropole which was located near the city center. After conferring with the hotel manager, Mr. Reilly took the microphone, read his list of designated roommates and handed out their room assignment cards as they left the bus.

"Off to bed," Mr. Reilly said. "We'll have a seven o'clock wake-up tomorrow. Breakfast at eight, and we leave at nine-thirty sharp. Don't be late."

The driver opened the luggage compartment and extracted the tightly packed bags. A few students pitched in to help unload the suitcases and handbags. Impatient to get to their rooms, the remaining students stood to the side and searched for their possessions. After claiming their bags, they quickly dragged them, and their tired bodies, through the hotel lobby toward the crowded single working elevator.

I tried to help Erin with her luggage, but she was already scurrying off with her assigned roommates dragging her bag behind her. No matter, I thought. I'll see her tomorrow. I joined my roommates, Mike Stevens and Billy Martin, the new guy from Denmark.

Crossing the lobby, we waited our turn at the tiny elevator. Many students ingeniously crammed their oversized bags and themselves into the tiny conveyance. The doors quietly closed time after time, and the old elevator creaked as it struggled to lift its heavy load. Soon it was our turn, and we repeated the ritual of squeezing into the small lift. We didn't say much as the elevator slowly rose to the fourth floor.

With a thud, the elevator abruptly stopped and the doors opened. There, in front of us, sat an elderly, heavy-set woman who worked as a Floor Lady. She was seated behind a small wooden desk, and managed a half smile while extending her hand for our room assignment cards. She wrote down the time that we arrived on a smudged page in a worn ledger that lay on her desk and then handed us our room key.

I later learned from Mr. Reilly that old retired women could supplement their meager pensions and earn a few extra rubles working as Floor Ladies. Their job was to issue and collect the room keys of hotel guests staying on their assigned floor each time a guest arrived or departed. I guess the cost and aggravation to replace a lost key was worth the small amount these women earned. It also gave them a job and some sense of respectability.

With our keys firmly in hand, we trudged down the poorly illuminated hall to our room. Three beds were lined against the drab walls. A small dresser and chest of drawers separated our limited living space. In the adjoining bathroom, a rustic shower dripped steadily. Mineral deposits stained the toilet bowl and small sink. White tiles, long since yellowed with age, covered the floor. Some floor tiles were either missing or cracked. Our one window opened to a view of an adjacent red-bricked building about 20 feet away.

Billy offered us first choice on the beds. He didn't say much and seemed older than Mike and me. It was almost as though he wasn't a student at all. He stayed to himself and appeared to be deep in thought. I tried to get him to loosen up some.

"What's it like in Lystrup, Billy? Have you always lived there?" I asked, trying to make conversation.

"Oh, it is cool and cloudy there. Town is small. Not much to do so I join TAP group to travel. Father never home. He work for Consulate there. I study in Europe but not so good the English. I hope you forgive my bad English."

"Oh, you speak good English. I can understand you."

"I speak Russian better," he continued.

That will be a big help, I thought. Speaking Russian will be handy when bartering for souvenirs. He seemed like a regular guy, yet mostly he kept to himself.

"Did you do any studying about this trip, Billy?" Mike joined in.

"Yuh. I take preparation courses by da mail while you go meetings each month in da States. I sit with Howie Bretton and Freddy Collins on plane ride from Sweden. They bring me up to date on what we do."

"Yuh, they are nice guys. Real photo nuts," Mike added. "You know, always taking pictures. I bet they've already gone through three rolls of film, and we haven't even started our tours."

"Yuh. They already take my picture on da plane too," Billy added.

"Must be tough meeting so many new faces all at once," I joined in.

"Oh, not so bad. You have nice girls in group too," Billy commented.

Billy seemed quite interested in the girls in our delegation and asked about some that he saw. We gladly filled him in, yet when he asked about the girl with the auburn hair, Erin, I tried to dodge his questions as skillfully as I could. After all, there were plenty of other girls he could meet. Trying to change the subject, I turned my attention to Mike.

"What are you goin' to do after high school, Mike?" I asked.

Mike was a senior at Granite High. He was an average sort of guy, with blond hair and hazel eyes. He said he joined the group at the urging of his parents. They traveled a lot, and he had picked up the 'travel bug' from them. Mike was as excited as anyone about the opportunity to travel, especially to Russia.

"I've been taking some college courses at night while still in high school. Maybe I'll get a job as a structural designer after college."

"Sounds like heavy stuff. What turned you on to that field?" I asked.

"Oh, my uncle keeps tellin' me about the developing opportunities in this field. I became quite interested in this work and read a lot of magazines on the subject."

"Good pay?" I asked.

"Yuh, they start you out high, and then it just goes up each year. You know, I wrote an article on futuristic buildings and submitted it to a magazine publisher but never heard back from them. They probably thought my ideas were too far out. Well, I still like designing things and I think I'd be good at it."

Mike said that his father wanted to expose him to foreign opportunities and urged him to do some overseas exploring to get a feel for other cultures.

"'Good learning experience,' my dad always said. Russia will open up soon and it's best to get in on the ground floor. So here I am," Mike continued.

It wasn't long before we climbed into our beds and wondered what surprises the morning would bring. Yawning, I pulled the sheets over my shoulder and closed my eyes. "Welcome to Moscow," I thought.

Chapter Five

The Kremlin

The morning sun and a gentle breeze seemed to play with the curtains swaying in the open window near the buffet table. The hotel dining room was especially busy at breakfast time. Besides the TAP delegation, there were many other guests. I could not tell if they were all Russians or tourists from surrounding countries. Not being familiar with any foreign language, I was at a loss. The most that I could hope for was a pleasant smile, or perhaps a nod to acknowledge their presence. We were told to always be polite and say good morning, but how do you say good morning when you don't know their language? Oh well, I suppose a smile and a nod would have to do.

The dining room furniture was old and worn from years of use. Some uneven tables were leveled with folded pieces of cardboard tucked under their legs. An old, glass chandelier hung in the center of the room providing the only light. It was dusty, and some of its bulbs had burned out. The floor was covered with a dark maroon carpet, which obviously had seen years of use, judging by its many threadbare areas.

The smell of crisp bacon and eggs filled the crowded room, as I slowly inched closer to the buffet tables. There were about twelve people ahead of me. Having eaten only airplane food in the past twenty-four hours, I wasted no time loading my plate to nearly overflowing from the tempting assortment of foods before me. I spotted an empty table in the corner, which provided an excellent vantage point from which to watch for Erin. I sat with my back to the wall, allowing me to see everyone entering the dining room. I was starved, and quickly tore into my breakfast, as I waited for Erin.

I knew that she must be someplace in the crowded dining room, but I couldn't see her. Maybe she had already finished breakfast, and had returned to her room, I thought. Trying not to be too obvious in my search, I decided to invite a couple of boys from our group to join me. Above the murmur of the students, we shared our impressions of our first day on foreign soil.

*****

The Sputnik motor coach rolled to a stop in the hotel parking area under the warm morning sun. Diesel exhaust fumes filled the air with dark black clouds of smoke. Oblivious to the diminishing amount of fresh air around them, the students in our delegation began to assemble near the bus, hoping to claim choice seats. Some fumbled with their cameras and day-bags, while others jealously guarded their large bottles of Coca-Cola.

I saw Erin near the front of the line that formed by the still-closed bus door. She was busy talking with another girl. I tried to work my way toward her, when a small band of street peddlers began approaching our group, looking for an opportunity to sell their pins, postcards, and matrioska (nesting) dolls. Billy was talking with one of the peddlers and nodding his head, as in agreement with something that the young scruffy peddler was saying. The other peddlers succeeded in making a few quick sales before being chased away by hotel security guards, only to reappear again the next day.

The bus doors finally opened, and the students scampered aboard claiming their seats for the day. I had wanted to sit with Erin, but she was already ahead of me in the queue. I knew she would save a seat for me, so I didn't try to push ahead. After parting company with the peddler, Billy wandered over to the bus, and waited near the door. Some admiring girls invited him to cut ahead of them in line. Before long, I, too, boarded the bus and headed down the aisle, looking for Erin. When I finally arrived at her seat, I saw that Billy had already claimed the adjoining seat for himself.

"I tried to save the seat for you, Jimmy, but Billy wanted to sit here to be close to the big window so he could take pictures while the bus was moving. I'm sorry."

"That's okay, Erin. I'll see you when we get to the Kremlin," I said half-heartedly.

Disappointed, as I had wanted to share this summer adventure with Erin, I took a seat at the rear of the coach. Billy was rapidly becoming a real thorn in my side.

Through the large window I saw Mr. Reilly walking quickly our way from the hotel. Mr. Reilly always walked very quickly, and I knew there was no emergency. He just wanted to start the day's activities without delay. The other two chaperones were already seated, and busy chatting in the front of the bus.

Mr. Reilly climbed aboard, and quickly started another of his many long head-counts.

"Thirty-six, thirty-seven, thirty-eight," he muttered to himself. "Looks like everyone is here," he shouted over the voices of the excited students.

A second head-count by Mrs. Kolinsky confirmed that everyone was indeed present.

"Nice job gang. I am very happy that everyone was so punctual. I hope you all brought plenty of film, as we'll visit a number of interesting places today."

With that, he gave a nod of his head to signal the driver that everyone was ready. Slowly the coach pulled away from the Metropole, and headed toward downtown Moscow, trailing a black cloud of pungent, choking fumes behind.

From where I was seated I could see that Billy and Erin were deep in conversation. Billy never did take a photo. I could see her laughing and the thought of Billy moving in on her made me increasingly angry. I had devoted much of my attention to Erin, and didn't really have any other close friends in the group. Oh yes, casual friendships, but nothing like the one I had with Erin. She was such a nice person, never judgmental, or condescending, and based on our conversations on the plane, I thought she liked me. Now, how could she be so quickly captivated by someone else? Maybe this was just a passing interest in Billy, and she would come back to me, I hoped.

Through the windows I could see the distant spires of the Kremlin's outer wall as the coach wormed its way through the busy city traffic. The rush hour was filled with many vintage cars that must be fifteen or twenty years old. Nearly all of them belched black sooty smoke that settled like an early morning fog over the downtown area.

"Look!" shouted one of the students. "McDonald's."

A spontaneous cheer erupted from everyone on the bus as we passed one of the two McDonald's Restaurants in Moscow. It was certainly a welcomed bit of home in this foreign setting.

"Can we stop there?" the students pleaded with Mr. Reilly.

"Maybe later," he replied.

Satisfied that his casual response could be considered a "yes," the students felt relieved and eagerly awaited their first burger and fries in Russia. Soon other familiar landmarks like Kentucky Fried Chicken, Baskin Robins, and pizza shops dotted the main thoroughfare. Almost like home, I thought.

"Look to da left," our tour guide announced. "Dis is da headquarters of the KGB...da Secret Police."

There it was - - a large ominous building standing at the far end of a main square. It was devoid of cars, people, or any form of activity. Thoughts of midnight knocks on the door, people dragged from their apartments, and cars speeding away with frightened occupants filled my mind. Perhaps these thoughts were only impressions I had from reading too many spy novels, but there it was, KGB Headquarters. Who can possibly know what kind of interrogation and torture actually took place in that dull, yellow colored, brick building? It was giving me the creeps to even think about it.

The Kremlin's main entrance.

Our bus stopped alongside a busy downtown thoroughfare. To the right was the Kremlin. A long cobbled stone bridge led to the entrance and the government buildings beyond. On the other side of the Kremlin Wall lay Red Square and Lenin's Mausoleum. A long line of people had already queued to enter Lenin's Tomb. I tried to reach Erin after we left the bus, but again she and Billy wandered ahead, still talking.

"Hey, Erin," I shouted. "Wait up."

"Hi, Jimmy. Billy and I were talking about the Kremlin. Have you had a chance to talk with Billy yet?"

"Yeah. We're crashing in the same room at the hotel. You know, roommates," I continued. "Hey, I thought we could spend some time together today."

"Oh, sure, you can hang out with Billy and me if you want."

"I mean just us two," I replied.

"Come on, Jimmy," Erin continued. "We can all get along, can't we?"

"What's the matter, Jimmy? Tryin' to squeeze me out?" Billy replied with a cold glance.

My opinion of Billy had now changed as I was seeing the confrontational side of him and didn't like it at all.

"No, but I'd like to spend more time with Erin without so much company around," I bravely retorted.

"Well, here she is. Take her, if you think you can," Billy shot back as he pushed me away.

Feeling the anger that had built up from early morning, I pushed him back and was ready for a fight. Billy stumbled backwards, falling to the pavement. He jumped back on his feet and lurched toward me when Erin ran between us, trying to keep us apart.

"Stop it, stop it. You two guys are acting like jerks," Erin screamed. "We can all have a good time together, if you just cool it." she yelled, trying to act as a mediator.

Erin was visibly shaken and started to cry. Although I didn't want any part of Billy, I reluctantly agreed to back off. Billy knew that he started the confrontation and was to blame. He, too, cooled down so as not to attract Mr. Reilly's attention. He seemed to be a year or two older than me. Maybe Erin liked older boys. Whatever could she see in Billy? Why doesn't she realize how much I really do care about her? I hoped Billy would find someone else to hang around with. Well, I was darn sure that I wasn't going to let him push me around. Erin was great in giving mixed signals, and now appeared not as interested in me as she had been on the airplane.

*****

Lenin's Tomb was in a small marble mausoleum next to a tall, brick wall that formed part of the perimeter of the Kremlin. Uniformed guards stood at the entrance to ensure a dignity befitting the leader of the Bolshevik Revolution and founder of the Communist state. Before visiting Lenin's Tomb, Mr. Reilly said that we would first visit other interesting places inside the Kremlin.

"Did you know that the word Kremlin means 'fortress' and that many towns in Russia had Kremlins," Mr. Reilly informed us.

"We are now in the Kremlin and our first stop will be at a museum dedicated to medieval weapons of the middle ages. Then we will tour the Congress of Deputies, where the Russian politicians meet," he continued.

Church of the Annunciation

It appeared that most students were only passively interested in these stops. Later in the day we toured the Church of the Annunciation where Ivan the Terrible attended services. Inside I saw the large enclosed wooden pew where he actually sat. The main church was quite large. It was supported by four massive columns and the walls were adorned with huge icons painted on wood. I was drawn to the two different Madonna and Child icons on opposite sides of the altar. This was a very impressive church, and I couldn't wait to share my interest with Erin.

"What do you think of that church, Jimmy?" Erin asked, as we walked down the steps and into an open courtyard.

"Oh, it was really impressive," I replied. "I loved the two Madonna and Child icons up by the altar. Also, that large wooden pew is where Ivan the Terrible actually sat for religious services. I've read about him in school but never paid much attention to his conquests. I bet the people really feared him."

"Yuh, he was da first Russian Czar and helped found Russia back in da 1500s. Smart man but very brutal too," Billy added. "Killed thousands of people up in Novgorod. He thought they were trying to overthrow him."

"Boy, he must have been paranoid. I'm glad I didn't live back then," Erin exclaimed.

After leaving the Church of the Annunciation we saw a huge church bell resting on a nearby sidewalk. Apparently it was never used. It had a large piece missing; two or three feet across. Our guide explained the significance of the bell but we arrived too late to hear his story. I guess I was still more concerned about Erin's sudden interest in Billy.

Slowly, we all headed toward Lenin's Mausoleum located just outside the Kremlin Wall. The tomb and the Kremlin Wall bordered one side of Red Square. On the opposite sides were the famous GUM department store and beautiful St. Basil's Cathedral. The square was very large and I recalled the television accounts of the many May Day parades held there. In contrast with more festive occasions, today the square was rather empty except for a long queue in front of the tomb and the tour buses neatly clustered on the opposite side of the square.

There it was, Lenin's final resting place. The mausoleum was flanked by two uniformed Army guards who stood rigidly at each corner. We joined the end of the long, snaking queue, as we waited for Mr. Reilly to return with our admission tickets. Shortly, he returned and instructed us to leave our cameras at the ticket office. No photographs were allowed inside the tomb, he said.

By making the tourists leave their cameras at the ticket office, Mr. Reilly said, the security people would be sure that no photos were taken. Apparently the flashes of the cameras would speed up the deterioration of Lenin's body. We dropped them off and again joined the line which had grown even longer. Surprisingly, the line did move rather quickly, and after a short 20-minute wait, we were entering the tomb.

It was chilly, dark, and rather spooky inside. Lenin's body lay in the center of a large room with a guard posted at each corner of the glass-covered casket, silently watching the line move along. No one was allowed to stop or say anything while in the tomb. The only sounds were the shuffling feet of the visitors who reverently paraded by. An odor of death filled the entombment chamber with its repugnant smell. Erin and Billy were ahead of me and I could see him whispering in her ear. Then they both smothered a silent chuckle. The guards didn't notice, which was lucky for them. The total silence added to the eerie pall over the inner chamber, and I couldn't wait to get out into the sunlight again.

Once outside, I asked them what they were laughing about. Erin could barely hold back her laughter. Once she regained her composure, she explained.

"Billy said that he thought he saw Lenin move. I nearly broke up. I'm glad that the guard didn't see me laughing."

"Yuh, you'd be in deep trouble for sure," I agreed. "A fine group of American ambassadors we'd be. They'd probably throw us out of the country on the next plane."

Actually, I, too, thought it was pretty funny and joined in their spontaneous laughter. I certainly couldn't accuse Billy of not having a sense of humor. He seemed to be a time bomb that could explode at anytime, yet I hoped that we could learn to be friends long enough to get through the rest of this week. I didn't trust him but would have to tolerate him, at least for the next few days. As we headed back to retrieve our cameras, we laughed and joked about our visit to the tomb.

Chapter Six

Suspicious Activity

The chime on the dusty grandfather's clock struck ten o'clock. I could hear it clearly as our group sat in the hotel lobby. Many students congregated there, as there was no other large area available where they could hang out. About twenty-five of our delegation filled the small lobby sitting on the floor or crowding around telephones chatting with their parents. I'm sure they were telling them about their visit to the Kremlin and Red Square. Other kids waited patiently for their turn to call home. They wouldn't be able to get through, however, as curfew was set for ten, and the old clock already tolled the end of the busy day. Many students drifted back to their rooms to chat with their roommates until the eleven o'clock bed-check. Mr. Reilly announced that he would take tonight's bed check, and that Mrs. Kolinsky and Mrs. Renaud would take turns on other nights.

"Did you enjoy today's activities, girls?" Mr. Reilly asked, as he quickly passed a small group who were returning to their rooms.

"Yeah" they replied excitedly. "What are we gonna do tomorrow?" they asked.

"Oh, I think we will be visiting Gorky Park. Seems as though there's a Russian Circus, and maybe, just maybe, we might be able to see it. Who knows, we might even find time to stop at a McDonald's, too."

"Yea! We're going to McDonald's," they yelled excitedly.

Mr. Reilly was very surprised and embarrassed by the youthful exuberance displayed by the girls over a mere visit to the 'Golden Arches'. He said nothing more, and quickly melted away into the shadows before someone saw him disturbing the tranquility of the lobby.

Shortly after eleven, there was a thumping knock on our door.

"Who is it?" I asked, knowing full well that it was our Delegation Leader.

Mr. Reilly had stressed over and over again that we should never open our hotel door without first verifying who was on the other side.

"Mr. Reilly," he replied.

With that deep voice, it was certainly him. I unlocked the door. His towering silhouetted figure nearly blocked the dim light from the hall ceiling.

"Let's see, you should have Billy and Mike in here with you, Jimmy."

Billy and Mike lay there on their beds and greeted Mr. Reilly.

"Okay, boys, don't forget that wake-up is at seven, breakfast at eight, and we are rolling at nine sharp. Don't be late."

"We won't. See you tomorrow, Mr. Reilly," I said, while slowly closing the door.

With that we settled in for a good night's rest as another busy day in Moscow lay ahead.

I don't know if it was all the Coke that I had been drinking during the day or the excitement of being so far from home, but I couldn't fall asleep. I lay there tossing and turning in my small single bed. A sliver of dim light slipped under the door. As I lay awake, my night vision allowed me to clearly see Billy and Mike who were sleeping nearby on the other side of the room.

I must have laid there for an hour trying to fall asleep. Suddenly, I saw Billy get out of bed and get dressed. Not knowing what he was up to, I decided to watch from the darkness while feigning sleep. What was he up to, I wondered. He quietly unlocked the door and the dim hall light outlined his every move. As he closed the door, I decided to stop him from breaking curfew and placing our group's whole trip in danger. I had to stop him. I quickly slipped into my clothes and followed him down the hall. The Floor Lady was not at her desk, long gone for the night. My curiosity grew, and I decided to watch his actions well out of sight. He crept slowly down the wide staircase. The desk clerk in the lobby dozed at his desk. Billy measured every step to avoid making any squeaking noises that would awaken the desk clerk. I felt more secure watching from above. From the second floor landing, I could see the lobby below. A bureau provided a very convenient hiding place for me to crouch out of sight.

From behind a tall, round pillar stepped the Russian peddler with whom I saw Billy talking earlier that morning. I couldn't hear what they were saying, except that I did catch a couple of words spoken in English. "Circus" and "money" were all I could understand. Billy and the Russian shook hands, and then Billy headed toward the staircase while the Russian slipped into the lobby's shadows. Not wishing to be seen spying on him, I quickly raced back to my room. My heart was beating loudly, and I feared that Billy would see me before I reached our room. Charging through the door, I jumped into bed without taking time to undress. Moments later Billy opened the door and went to bed. He hadn't seen me in the hallway and was unaware that he was being watched. Perhaps it was best not to tell Mr. Reilly of Billy's midnight rendezvous because he would be very upset and might even send Billy back home. Thoughts of this mysterious encounter continued to race through my mind, keeping me awake for quite awhile. Eventually I drifted off to sleep.

*****

"Good morning, guys" Mike exclaimed cheerfully. "Looks like another nice day. Can't wait to get going. I understand that we're going to a circus today. Hope the bus is on time."

"Yuh, me too" I replied still half asleep.

Actually, I was more interested in what was going to happen at the circus with my roommate and his Russian peddler friend. Billy had climbed out of bed and hadn't spoken a word to either Mike or me. I was growing more suspicious of Billy. He didn't seem to fit in, and he was almost disinterested in what our group was here for. What was he trying to accomplish? I knew I had to keep a close watch on him today.

"What did you think of Lenin's Tomb, Jimmy?" Mike inquired.

Mike was eager to start a conversation, although my mind was on Billy's secret activities. His silence was all too apparent as we walked to breakfast. He didn't say a word as Mike and I talked about Lenin's Tomb, Gorky Park and the circus. Something seemed to weigh heavily upon Billy, yet I didn't want to let him know that I was aware of his sudden friendship with the Russian peddler or of his midnight rendezvous.

Erin was sitting alone at the end of a long table on the side of the musty dining room and we decided to join her. The one redeeming feature of this hotel was its great food. The hotel, although old, and not well maintained, did serve many foreign guests; and the food was always good and plentiful. Today I decided to sample some of the typical Russian fare, while Erin opted for some fruit and pastry. Billy and Mike followed us through the line as they, too, made their selections.

Apparently realizing that he hadn't spoken a word all morning, Billy inquired, "How ist da fruit, Erin?"

"Great. Do you want to try some?" she asked, while sliding her plate toward him.

"No, thanks. Say, Erin, what do ya say 'bout going on da Ferris Wheel or some other ride with me at Gorky Park?"

"Gee, that sounds great, Billy," she said, while smiling and gently wiping her lips with her napkin.

"Maybe we could be alone at da park and not hang out with anyone. What do ya say?"

"Maybe," she replied.

This was an obvious attempt to exclude both Mike and myself. He was making a play for Erin, and I wasn't going to give her up that easily. Maybe this was payback time for my attempt to spend time alone with her in Red Square yesterday. Accepting his friendship was one thing, but now I wished that he had never come on this trip. Could Erin be so blinded by his obvious advances toward her? Why doesn't she realize how much I care for her? She'd change her mind if she knew that he broke curfew last night and had secret meetings in the middle of the night. Yet that could ruin the trip for everyone. Maybe if I told her she would dump him and prefer to be my friend rather than his. No, I couldn't run the risk of having her tell Mr. Reilly and besides, Billy would only deny it. Who would believe such a wild story anyway? I must wait, I thought. Maybe something more concrete would develop at Gorky Park.

"What are you thinking about, Jimmy?" Erin asked.

I must have been in a trance or maybe didn't get enough sleep last night, and it was being noticed.

"Oh, uh, nothing," I said.

Just then Billy and Mike excused themselves and headed to the buffet table for second helpings. I now saw my chance to speak openly to Erin about my feelings and suspicions.

"Erin, I hope you know that I really like you. It bothers me to see that new guy, Billy, trying to monopolize you and squeeze me out."

"Yes, I know, Jimmy. You're a nice guy and I like you too. Still, we should be more accepting of Billy. It's not his fault that he wants a friend. He is all alone, you know."

"Yuh, but does he have to be so pushy?"

"He's not pushy. Maybe it's just the way he was brought up. You know, living in Europe all his life," she continued. "We can all be friends and have a super time. Give it a little time, Jimmy."

"Okay, but I still don't trust him."

I wanted to let Erin in on what I knew about Billy, yet I hesitated, not knowing just how much to say. Certainly she would think I was making it all up just to get some kind of revenge. I would tell her at some point, but I would need to know more about Billy's activities first.

Just then Mike and Billy returned with their second helpings of food. We talked a while longer about our impressions of Moscow.

From his seat which faced the slightly opened window, Mike saw the large blue and white Sputnik bus rolling into the hotel parking area.

"Let's hurry and get some good seats," Mike blurted.

"Okay. First, I have to get some more film. Save me a seat," I told the three of them and quickly headed for the hotel newsstand.

The last of the students climbed aboard the bus as I ran to catch up. Working my way down the aisle, I could see Billy and Erin seated together again. Darn! They were both carrying on. She was obviously enjoying his company. Mike had saved a seat for me and I resigned myself to the fact that I would have to find some way to win Erin back from Billy's advances.

Mr. Reilly again squeezed down the narrow aisle counting heads. "Thirty five, thirty six, thirty seven, thirty eight. Good," he mumbled to himself. Mrs. Kolinsky also did her double count. Satisfied that they had everyone, Mr. Reilly gave thumbs up to the driver. Again, a big puff of black, choking smoke belched from under the bus as it rolled out of the hotel parking lot and into the morning traffic.

Mr. Reilly clicked on the microphone, and after turning the volume up to the maximum, he accidentally sneezed. A loud roar thundered throughout the bus. Frightened students abruptly fell silent, and surrendered their attention to the tall commanding figure at the front. Realizing the fear and panic he had created, Mr. Reilly and the students together broke into laughter.

"Today, gang," he said, "we will take a two hour boat ride on the Moscow River, past the Kremlin, and eventually stop on the other side of the river. That's where Gorky Park is located. You are free to wander in the park but you must not leave it. We will all meet at one o'clock by the large carousel that lies in the center of the park and then walk to the circus. Don't be late," he stressed.

Mr. Reilly sat back and laughed with the other leaders about his powerful opening announcement.

As the coach wound its way down the pot-holed boulevard toward the Moscow River, we again passed McDonald's as another cheer filled the coach. Mr. Reilly sensed that this outburst was an obvious reminder of his promise to find time today to visit this American icon. He waved his hand in the air without turning around, to indicate that a visit was indeed on the agenda. The students smiled and laughed at his method of acknowledging their wishes.

We continued through the traffic which was now backed up and creeping slowly. We drove by Moscow University and Serge took the opportunity to tell us about the programs of study offered there. The university building was massive and we were very impressed. Serge then announced that we were almost at the boat landing and that they were waiting for us.

The bus eventually slowed to a crawl in the heavy morning traffic. Heavy black exhaust fumes encircled the rear section and poured into the half-opened windows. Many students began coughing and gagging on the noxious air. A moment later the bus inched its way forward, through the crowded intersection, and the air slowly began to clear. Some students were still wiping tears from their eyes as the bus eventually reached the river's edge.

"Okay, everyvun, stay together. Follow me," Serge said in his broken accent.

We trailed behind him to a waiting boat that reminded me of an old ferry that I had seen on Lake Champlain. Dirty, white paint was flaking off, and the deck was spotted with many years of grease stains. Carefully, we climbed up the rickety gangplank, as the boat attendant counted each person passing by. Once the numbers were firmly fixed, Serge bought tickets and before long he, too, was onboard. The old boat churned up the muddy waters under the transom and pulled away from the pier, moving slowly up the broad river.

Moscow University.

I joined Erin and Billy on the upper deck while Mike met some other friends below. We watched the Kremlin buildings and the traffic moving slowly along the shore. On the opposite side, the towering Moscow University dominated the skyline. Billy and Erin leaned against the ship's railing and commented on the Moscow buildings that lay before them. Billy slid his arm around Erin's waist. Although initially startled, she didn't seem to object. Again, I felt helpless and left out, but could do nothing. It seemed that Erin was trying to be a friend to both of us, however, I seemed to be on the losing end.

"Billy, what are you doing?" she asked, as she pulled his arm away. "You know that Mr. Reilly might catch us."

"Yuh," I blurted out defiantly. "You're going to get Erin in trouble and ruin the whole trip for all of us," I added, feeling more and more hostility toward Billy.

"Okay, okay. I guess I'm out-numbered, but what Erin and I do is none of your business, so stay clear," he snarled my way.

I knew that our animosity was growing and would certainly reach a boiling point soon if we continued our jabs at each other. I decided to back off and let things subside some.

Apparently feeling a bit nervous, Erin pulled away from Billy. I guess she felt uncomfortable and maybe a bit scared that Mr. Reilly would catch them. After all, he had told us many times at the TAP meetings that he would not tolerate any hanky-panky or puppy love on this adventure.

Our two-hour boat ride provided ample opportunity to take many pictures of the Moscow buildings and city scenes. Before long, we were docking at Gorky Park and had the freedom to wander wherever we wanted. Dirt paths and occasional water-filled potholes were framed with tall, uncut grass. Small birds darted in and out of the water, fluttering their wings to wash their feathers. A shower during the night had filled the depressions in the uneven paths, turning them into impromptu birdbaths during the day.

Along the way we passed many small kiosks, listening to vendors hyping games of chance or selling souvenirs, cotton candy, and soda. Through a clearing in the trees we saw a small, manmade lake dotted with a few tourists in paddleboats sharing the waters with swans. On the opposite side, ducks quacked and scrambled for bits of bread thrown their way. Billy's eyes were focused on the Ferris Wheel that loomed in the distance. I recalled his offer to take Erin on that ride and wished that I could take her instead. Maybe I will, I thought, as I gathered enough courage to ask her. I didn't know how Billy would react and really didn't care.

"Say, Erin, would you like to go on the Ferris Wheel with me?" I bravely asked.

"Hey, I asked her first," Billy blurted loudly. This time I could sense Billy's anger and in spite of it, I defiantly I repeated my question.

"What do you say, Erin?"

"Now, now, I can go on the ride with both of you," she said, while again trying to act as both a mediator and referee.

I was quite relieved when I saw that the Ferris Wheel's seats could only hold two people at a time. I would, at last, have her to myself for a short time, I thought.

Billy took her on the ride first and I could see him putting his arm around her and sitting very close. She didn't seem to object, knowing that Mr. Reilly would not see them. The old amusement creaked and rocked in the late morning sunshine. Feelings of anger and jealousy were overtaking me, but I patiently waited until the ride was over. Next, it was my turn and I relished the thought of sitting close to her and hopefully winning her back. The big wheel creaked and groaned as it slowly turned, lifting us higher and farther away from Billy, who leaned patiently against a metal fence below. Now, at last, I had Erin to myself.

The wooden seat was quite narrow, and her body was crowded closely against mine. With each rocking motion the large wheel climbed ever higher to its lofty perch. I could feel the warmth of Erin's soft arms and body next to mine. Thoughts of how she snuggled up to me on the airplane flashed through my mind. It seemed so right. I felt my heart pounding inside and hoped that Erin could sense my love and concern. I knew that I had to have Erin, but what should I do about Billy? I wanted to ask her what she saw in him but didn't have the courage to bring up the subject. Besides, I was enjoying being so close and seeing her enjoying herself so much.

A sudden gust of wind blew her loose blouse tightly against her chest and the outline of her firmly rounded breasts aroused feelings that I hadn't experienced before. She held her head high as a warm breeze caught her long flowing hair, blowing it across her face. She laughed and brushed it aside, gently holding it away from her eyes. Without saying a word, she looked at me and squeezed my hand as if to indicate her feelings. Her apparent signal seemed to give me the inner strength to finally ask her about Billy.

"Erin, why do you spend so much time with Billy and why do you let him put his hands all over you?" I said before realizing how blunt the question was.

"What?" she snipped. "I don't. And what he does is none of your business," she replied angrily.

I was caught off-guard by her sudden and unexpected reply, yet I also realized how inappropriate and ill mannered my question was.

"Besides, he is nice, so I don't know why it should bother you. I can pick my own friends without any help from you," she snapped back.

I knew that I had blown it and was rapidly losing ground. We sat without talking until the big wheel finally slowed to a stop. Erin jumped from the chair to the platform and rushed awkwardly down the walkway to where Billy was waiting. I followed behind and said nothing to further annoy her. He had already bought her a hot dog and soda. As they wandered up the path, I quickly bought something to eat and hurried to catch up.

It was nearly time for our one o'clock meeting with Mr. Reilly at the carousel. Ahead of us lay a big yellow tent just beyond the carousel. Soon we would enjoy a Russian Circus. Oh yes, the circus. Thoughts of last night's secret meeting again raced through my mind. What might happen at the circus?

Chapter Seven

The Circus

The sounds of organ music filled the air as we arrived at the carousel. I found the music very similar to the tunes I've heard many times before. The carousel played on and on, while we waited for our group to assemble. Mr. Reilly, meanwhile, stood off to the side and checked his notes, oblivious to the music that filled the afternoon air.

As I waited, my mind drifted off to times long before. The organ music reminded me of the big merry-go-round at the Canobie Lake Park entrance. Yes, that's it, Canobie Lake Park. My parents said that they liked to visit the park in the old days and to bring picnic lunches with them. You can't do that now. Times are changing. Everything is much more commercialized. The park is still in operation, and it continues to be a very popular attraction during warmer months. I imagined that Gorky Park must be like the old Canobie Lake Park that my folks had visited.

From the carousel in the center of Gorky Park, paths led out like spokes of a wheel. Down each path you could find various concessions, amusement rides, rowing ponds, gardens, and even a large Big Top circus.

By my count, we now had thirty-six students. I could see that Mr. Reilly was becoming impatient, as he waited for the two missing kids. While we waited, some students climbed on the carousel and enjoyed the music and the vividly painted wooden horses that alternately rose and fell. The students laughed and chattered above the loud organ grinder tunes, as the merry-go-round spun around and around.

Many Russian families visited the park with their children. Some pushed baby strollers while others brought older kids who wanted to try every ride. The day's warm, summer weather had brought out a large number of park visitors. Many seemed curious about the American students scampering about in their shorts and jeans. Unlike them, we were quite boisterous in our activities.

Most locals dressed rather discretely. The men and women wore darker conservative clothing even in summer. Some women also wore a colorful kerchief as well. They didn't seem to smile much, but otherwise they enjoyed their visit to the park. The children wore colorful clothes and were also bundled up for the unpredictable Moscow weather. Today's sunny weather belied the fact that showers were predicted for the late afternoon.

In the distance, I could see Melanie and Rachel running in our direction. They arrived shortly, huffing and puffing. When they reached Mr. Reilly, they stopped, trying to catch their breaths, before explaining their tardiness.

"My watch battery died, and I didn't know the time," Rachel confessed. "I tried to ask a Russian family but couldn't make myself understood."

They were very apologetic and Mr. Reilly forgave them with a stern warning. He then winked at them, and the girls felt relieved that they were back in his good graces. Mr. Reilly was good, like that, and the kids really liked him.

"Okay, everyone, gather 'round," Mr. Reilly shouted over the organ music. "I hope you all had something to eat because we are now heading for the circus. Before we go, however, I need to count heads again. Of course, I am sure that's no surprise to anyone," he added with a slight smile.

With that, he started his headcount. Satisfied with having the magic number of thirty-eight, he led the procession down the path to the big yellow tent.

As we strolled along, I could see the circus performers rehearsing their acts behind the large canvas tent. Elephants patiently waited along side small dogs, while clowns carefully applied final layers of make-up before small mirrors. Circus helpers tugged on ropes, securing them to stakes. A small monkey jumped through his trainer's hoop, landing on his front hands and rolling over. He stopped upright and immediately jumped up and down clapping his hands and yakking as if to show approval for his own performance. We laughed to see such unabashed pride.

"Did you see that?" Erin yelled. "That monkey feels pretty proud of himself, don't you think?"

"Yuh, he mimics the audience for they always cheer such acts," Billy joined in.

"Bet ya he's been at it for quite some time. Kinda routine for him, doin' it everyday," I said.

Melodious pipe organ music again filled the air with a gaiety and excitement as if to announce the dazzling acts that were soon to follow. I could smell the scent of fresh popcorn that permeated the air and hear the excited voices of small children long before reaching the big tent. To the left of the big top were many wagons that appeared to be used for make-up and props. One was painted with bright splashes of red, yellow, and blue. Bold Cyrillic letters were painted on its sides near a picture of a tiger with open mouth and sharp teeth.

Standing by one of the wagons, nearly concealed by the shadows created by the afternoon sun, I saw a tall man slowly re-light a half burned cigarette that barely clung to his lips. In the glare of his match, I immediately recognized him. This was the peddler who had met Billy at the hotel last night. This same man was somehow involved with Billy, but I couldn't piece the puzzle together. Billy also saw this man and paused for a moment, but apparently decided to remain with Erin and myself. He knew he couldn't leave the group with Mr. Reilly standing nearby.

Serge purchased tickets for us and briefly chattered with the attendant. He then pointed to his watch, and the attendant nodded as he continued his conversation. Billy again glanced nervously back toward the wagon, this time making eye contact with the scruffy lone figure leaning against a trailer. A brief nod and the figure disappeared. Erin was preoccupied trying to untangle her hair that had become hopelessly snarled earlier in the brisk afternoon breezes. I pretended not to notice Billy's actions and hoped that my curiosity would not become too apparent. Billy nervously dropped the ticket that Serge had just given him. He picked it up and brushed aside the sawdust.

"I'm in Row 9 Seat 5. Where is your seat?" I asked Erin.

"I'm in Row 9, Seat 6," she casually replied.

"Hey, that's next to me. Billy, where's your seat?" I asked.

Glancing at his ticket, he replied, "Oh, uh, I'm on da aisle in Row 8," he muttered without much concern.

He seemed to have his mind set on other things, perhaps the stranger he had seen outside. I was just as glad that he was not in our row. Maybe I could somehow work back into Erin's good graces without having Billy butt in, I thought.

The chatter and excitement continued until the large, center single ring tent was nearly filled. Some American students searched for enough rubles to make their last minute purchase of survival foods, like soda and unshelled peanuts. Russian children seemed to crave the same circus fare and eagerly tugged at their mother's dresses to emphasize their desires. Slowly the mothers counted the small number of coins needed and handed their meager savings to the vendor. He counted the kopeks and promptly handed a small bag of peanuts to the impatient child. Other parents seemed relieved when the music again started after a pause. They leaned over and whispered something into their child's ear. Perhaps it was to tell them that the show was about to begin. Maybe it was some other believable way to get the child away from the vendor and save what little money they had. There would always be other opportunities to treat their child to some summer delight, I thought.

The air was filled with a slight musty odor that one would expect with the many animals that performed day after day in the same setting. One large fan at the far end of the tent churned, in vain, small amounts of air. Fresh sawdust was always spread on any animal droppings, but apparently they were cleaned up only periodically. Pipe organ music filled the enclosed tent with a loudness that almost drowned out any chance for conversation. The music was lively and added to the enthusiasm and expectations of the eager crowd.

I could see Billy in the row below me. He was searching the audience very intently and made no attempt to look our way or speak to the boy sitting beside him. I continued to keep an eye on him, as something was surely to happen during the circus. I just knew it.

Erin apparently had forgotten my abruptness earlier in the day as she smiled at me and tried to find some comfort in her hard wooden seat. The rows were quite close together. This made for some cramped legs which added to the overall discomfort of the spectators. We were seated near the middle of the large tent and could clearly see the spectators' entrance at one end and the performers' entrance at the other. Erin didn't speak much as she was busy studying the colorful panorama that lay before her.

"This is really exciting, don't ya think?" she blurted to me.

I felt a sense of relief as we were hopefully on speaking terms again.

"Yuh, this is really neat. Hey look, here comes the Ringmaster," I replied.

From the far end I could see the Ringmaster dressed in a colorful red and white uniform. He carefully placed a tall black hat on his head and headed toward the single center ring. Along the way he paused with arms up-reached for a second or two in front of the large fan, seemingly to savor some fresh air before his duties started under the glare of the hot spotlights. The general lighting had already been dimmed. The hot afternoon sun added its heat to the body heat of nearly 800 people in the circus audience. The still air was stifling, which increased the restlessness of the spectators. In an effort to reduce the overwhelming temperatures inside the tent, circus helpers began to roll up some of the tent flaps behind the bleachers. Cooler air from a nearby grove slid under the rolled-up flaps and brought some relief.

Two bright overhead spotlights followed the Ringmaster to center ring where he apparently welcomed everyone to 'the greatest show on earth.' Of course, he spoke in Russian. A large applause followed his speech in which he apparently described some of the acts that were to follow.

The opening spectacle involved a parade of beautiful white horses that charged around the inside of the tent and then into the central ring. They reared their bodies up and placed their front hooves on the horse ahead, then pranced around the ring to the delight of all.

The following acts involved trained dogs and then cats. Dogs happily jumped through hoops, even a flaming one, held by their trainer. Afterwards, two trained cats were coaxed onto large balls. They walked them around the ring. I was very impressed with the cats, as I had never seen a cat perform before. Erin was also thrilled with the stunts and enjoyed herself in spite of the unbearable heat.

"What'd yuh think of that cat act?" I asked Erin. "I've never seen a cat perform before."

"I wonder how they actually train cats to perform. They are very independent creatures and seldom follow any directions," she said.

"They must spend a lot of time training them. Then there are no guarantees that they will do their thing when the show starts."

I frequently glanced in Billy's direction and noticed that he also seemed to enjoy the circus routines. My attention again returned to Erin as we commented on each event that followed.

During one of the applauses, I glanced to my left to focus on Billy. A cold chill overtook me; he was gone. I frantically searched the crowd without luck. A few children scurried toward the roaming vendors or the outside portable toilets. There, near the exit opening, I caught a glimpse of Billy as he disappeared around some sound equipment and circus props. I knew that I had to follow him and I whispered to Erin that I had to use the portable toilet outside. She nodded that she understood. With repeated apologies, I clumsily crawled over the students in our row, raced down the rickety planks two at a time, and scampered toward the same opening where I last had seen Billy.

Fresh air and milder temperatures offered a welcomed coolness in contrast to the overwhelming heat inside the tent. Aside from a few children waiting for the portable toilets, I could see no one. Where could have Billy disappeared, I wondered.

This side of the big yellow tent was crowded with small house trailers where circus performers and trainers apparently lived. I slowly wandered from trailer to trailer, not knowing if I would find Billy or if he would find me. What would I say if he saw me first?

Just as I was about to give up searching and head back to the Big Top, I recognized Billy's voice coming from the other side of an old green trailer next to me. I crouched down and saw two people on the opposite side of the trailer. Carefully, I crawled under the trailer on my hands and knees and saw all that was happening. I was well hidden behind the trailer wheels. I clearly heard more than I wanted to hear. I lay there in disbelief.

Chapter Eight

The Rendezvous

Billy appeared quite nervous. Beads of sweat rolled from the sides of his face. His voice was shaky, and he apparently wanted to finish his business with the Russian peddler as quickly as possible.

"You got it?" the peddler demanded.

"What?"

"Da money," the peddler again demanded with more determination.

"Yuh. Here it is," Billy said while pulling a small brown paper envelope from his pants pocket and handing it to the impatient peddler.

The peddler quickly counted the money and then said, "OK. Here's what you want."

He handed Billy a small envelope which he tore open. Inside was a small piece of paper which Billy skimmed over before tucking it into his pants pocket.

"Dis better be real or else we're going to meet again, and it won't be a pleasant meeting," Billy said coldly.

"Yuh, yuh. Dis ist no lie. I do vat you want. Don't worry. You don't be late either. Mr. Kastrovna don't like to wait."

A short conversation followed and then the Russian peddler quickly scurried off behind a circus wagon. Billy turned while slipping the small paper into his pocket. He then made his own hurried departure toward the sounds of nearby applause and familiar pipe organ music.

After brushing the dirt and sawdust from my clothes, I hurried back to the circus tent with a thousand thoughts now racing through my mind. I was afraid that Billy might suspect me of spying on him if he saw me. What would I say to Erin after my long absence? After all, I had told her that I was just going to the toilet. I hoped that Mr. Reilly wouldn't see me wandering away from the circus. Should I tell Mr. Reilly what I saw? I knew I should, but he'd never believe me. After all, Billy would just deny it and it would be his word against mine. I was confused as these rambling thoughts raced through my mind. Stopping, I glanced up at the gaily decorated tent before me with its flags and streamers fluttering in the afternoon breeze.

I slipped under the yellow canvas side flaps. The trapped heat was intense and nearly knocked me over. Drops of sweat began to drip from my forehead as I made my way past concessions and spectators. I had to return to my seat as inconspicuously as possible. Passing a food vendor, I decided to buy Erin a bag of popcorn. Billy wouldn't become suspicious if I headed back to my seat with a bag of popcorn. Besides, I might make a few points with Erin as well. I counted my rubles and found that I had enough for two bags of popcorn. Might as well enjoy some too, I thought. I raised two fingers and handed my small fortune to the smiling vendor. He happily acknowledged my thank you with a wide grin. I turned again toward the long row of crowded bleachers where Erin sat and watched each amazing circus act. Slowly I pushed my way through the crowded tent and up the rickety steps.

The audience had their eyes glued on the acrobats who spun and leaped from bar to bar high above the appreciative crowd. Woos and ahs could be heard as each leap became more death defying and challenging. I was missing the main event and hurried up the bleacher aisle passing Billy who sat with a blank look on his face. It was obvious that he wasn't paying any attention to the acrobatic acts taking place above him. He never did make eye contact with me, and I was just as happy that he didn't.

Again, I had to crawl over four students before reaching my seat. Erin saw me coming and wondered where I had been for such a long time. I told her that there had been a line waiting to use the portable toilets. This was true, but I didn't tell her that I hadn't been in that line.

Trying to change the subject, I whispered to her "Here's something I bought for you, Erin."

The buttery popcorn brightened her eyes and brought a big smile to her face as she squeezed my hand.

"Gee, thanks, Jimmy. It's just what I wanted. You are really thoughtful, aren't you?" she replied.

A sense of relief overtook me, and I again felt very comfortable with my rebounding romance. She enthusiastically told me all about some of the events that I had missed.

"Jimmy, you missed a really super act when the elephants paraded around the ring. A baby elephant wandered away and its mother left the line and herded him back without being prodded. The Ringmaster just stood there in disbelief, and the crowd applauded for a long time. I guess a mother's instinct takes over even here in a circus tent," Erin chuckled.

"Gee, I would have liked to have seen that. Guess I left at the wrong time."

My eyes were still fixed on Billy who sat nervously re-reading the small note he had received earlier. The trapeze acrobatics soon ended, and were followed by a loud tumultuous applause from a delighted audience.

With the final performance over, the performers, trainers, and animals again paraded around the large tent and through the center ring to the standing applause of hundreds of satisfied spectators. The large tent emptied slowly. Our group meandered back to the carousel that had been our previous rendezvous point.

I could see Mrs. Kolinsky and Mrs. Renaud laughing, apparently quite satisfied with today's leisurely pace and impressive circus performance. Mrs. Renaud proudly sported a large, red felt hat with flashing lights around its brim. She bought the circus souvenir during the intermission and hid it in her shoulder bag until now. The students in our group laughed when she turned the lights on and quickly followed her single file as if in a parade. Mrs. Kolinsky even jumped into the "conga line" amidst the laughter of the happy wanderers from America.

"Come on, Mr. Reilly, jump in," the kids begged, but he was very reserved and kept his distance, although he quietly laughed. He then encouraged some other kids to join the line even though he wouldn't.

As the happy procession wormed its way down the path toward the carousel, Russian families smiled in approval. Throwing their coats aside, Russian children exuberantly joined our spontaneous line.

Carousel music blared in the distance and became louder with each twist and turn of our wild procession. Mr. Reilly walked quickly to keep up with the energetic high-steppers that he had volunteered to lead. Erin and I were near the front of the 'Pied Piper' parade and laughed so much that our stomachs' began to hurt. This jovial procession would certainly become the highlight of our day at Gorky Park. At last, we arrived at the carousel, and all but a couple of students clustered in a circle waiting for the daily ritual of Mr. Reilly's 'nose counting.' I could see Billy lagging behind Mr. Reilly, alone and deep in thought. One could easily see that he was quite troubled and nervous. This sudden change was in stark contrast to his macho behavior earlier in the day.

I knew that I must inform Mr. Reilly and decided to tell him right then and there. I told Erin that I would be right back and walked over to him as he approached the waiting group.

"Mr. Reilly, do you have a minute?" I blurted, almost without thinking.

"Sure, Jimmy, what is it?" he replied in a concerned fatherly way.

At this moment I realized that I had only my suspicions about the events that I had seen earlier. Billy might have long since ditched that note he received back at the circus wagon. Mr. Reilly was an impatient man and wouldn't believe me with such flimsy information. Maybe I should just follow Billy some more before I told anyone, I thought.

"Well, what is it?" Mr. Reilly again asked. I could see that he wanted to start counting the students who stood nearby.

"I, ah…. oh, nothing."

I would tell him, but I would wait until I had more evidence. Suspicions just wouldn't do. Mr. Reilly then turned and started his counting.

"Thirty-six, thirty-seven, thirty-eight."

He was now satisfied with his count and didn't even wait for Mrs. Renaud to complete hers before he started walking down the winding dirt walkway toward the boat landing. The students followed closely behind. The crimson sun slid behind the tall chestnut trees casting long shadows along the pathway. Chilling late afternoon breezes and darkening skies signaled the approach of the predicted showers.

Erin and I chattered about some of the animal acts that we enjoyed. Excitedly, she described other events that I had missed. I was glad that she didn't quiz me on where I had gone for such a long time. I didn't want to lie to her. Still, I couldn't tell her the truth either.

A quiet boat ride back across the meandering Moscow River gave everyone a chance to unwind. The morning's excitement and clamor had mellowed into serene afternoon reflections. Some students tried to keep a running journal while others reported the day's activities into small portable tape recorders. Both groups were anxious to record the daily events to later share with their parents.

I could see our Sputnik coach on the opposite shore next to an old brown shack that was used as an office by the boat company. Once moored, the students slowly dragged themselves up the uneven gangplank and wandered over to the bus. The ride back to the Hotel Metropole was quite relaxing as we gazed out the windows at the passing cityscape.

Shoppers headed home with long loaves of bread tucked under their arms. Some carried small packages wrapped in newspapers tied with strings. Perhaps they hid a bottle of vodka to provide some relief from the day's drudgery, I thought. I didn't see many smiling faces and few signs of happiness or contentment. Russian life was neither easy nor carefree. Discretionary spending enjoyed by many Americans was not to be found in Russia. They lived from hand to mouth with little thought about the carefree days of retirement and leisure. They had depended on the government for work, housing, medical care, and security. Now with the fall of Communism and the collapse of the Soviet Union, there were no guarantees and little hope for a better tomorrow.

Our Sputnik coach slowed and turned into a small street in a commercial area of downtown Moscow and stopped.

"What are we stopping for?" the students asked one another.

We all thought that we were heading back to the hotel and were surprised by this unexpected, yet welcomed, stop.

Mr. Reilly clicked on the microphone and said that Mrs. Kolinsky had an announcement. He handed her the microphone.

"Boys and girls, instead of eating at the hotel tonight, the leaders thought everyone might enjoy dinner at McDonald's. We will…"

A large cheer erupted and echoed throughout the bus drowning out her last sentence. The students were thrilled to visit this little American island here in the heart of Moscow. They scampered out of the bus and there, around the corner, stood the 'Golden Arches.'

This McDonald's was different from those in the United States, however. A guard stood at the door to deter vagrants and homeless people from entering. They wanted to maintain a clean wholesome atmosphere, it seemed. The guard smiled and held the door open for our large group to enter. Inside was a long serving counter with many servers franticly waving their hands high in the air to indicate that they were available to take orders. I later learned that they were told to do this to assure speedy and friendly service. The menu was similar to that back home. There were no tables to sit at, yet there were a few stools that encircled brightly colored pillars. We left these free for our chaperones. There were plenty of clean counters where diners stood and ate their meals.

Mike joined us in ordering combination meals. While sinking our teeth into this unexpected treat, we compared this restaurant to those at home. Billy tested each bite and also offered his approval. Erin liked the familiar atmosphere and the feeling of being close to home again. For me, I also gave a thumbs-up as I inhaled my meal.

The three chaperones joined the students as they, too, enjoyed their meals yet in a slower, and more dignified manner with napkins in hand. Mr. Reilly seemed to especially savor the ambiance and familiar surroundings of this home away from home. He then chattered some more with the two women.

"Tomorrow we will visit a Russian Army camp. Maybe we can get some of these boys to enlist," he chuckled.

Mrs. Kolinsky and Mrs. Renaud laughed, while nodding their heads, and continued slowly sipping their cold drinks.

After the meal, we again climbed aboard the idling coach and quietly waited the results of the headcount and double check. Mr. Reilly passed this chore off to the two women who were quite proficient at it. One started from the front and the other from the rear of the bus. Everyone broke out in laughter as they passed mid-way. Considering their sizes, they could barely squeeze by one another. Mr. Reilly stood at the front and watched the struggle taking place as the two women tried their best to navigate the narrow aisle. He slowly shook his head from side to side while a broad grin belied his somber demeanor.

"Let's roll," he finally called out and the bus slowly eased out onto the main city street and eastward toward the hotel.

Before long, the oversized coach pulled into the dimly lit hotel parking area, enveloped by ever-present diesel fumes, just as a bell on some distant church struck eight. The students had long since lost their exuberance and slowly dragged themselves from the bus, across the parking area toward the hotel entrance. Security guards dutifully waited as we approached with souvenirs in tow. Erin paired off with one of her female friends while Mike and I recalled some of the circus stunts as we walked along. Billy quietly ambled along alone and appeared to be deep in thought.

"Velcome. Velcome," the security guards repeated as they greeted the weary students and held the doors wide open.

It seemed that this was the only English word they knew. Most students thanked them and sauntered through the lobby toward the elevators and up to their rooms.

Mike and I were tired and decided not to hang out in the Game Room as we had planned. A good night's rest seemed much more appealing. As we waited for the elevator, I saw Billy making a telephone call at the far end of the lobby. My curiosity again got the better of me and I decided to hang around the lobby to see what I might learn.

"Mike, I think I'll check out that newsstand near the phones. Maybe get a candy bar or somethin'. You head on up, and I'll catch up with you shortly."

"Want me to go with you?" he asked.

"No, no. You take off. I'll be right along," I replied.

"Okay. See you up in the room."

With that, Mike headed through the open elevator doors. I watched as they closed. The visible sliver of light between the doors soon faded into darkness as the elevator slowly rose.

I now turned my attention to Billy who was still talking on the telephone. How is it that he spoke such good Russian for a person who was brought up in Denmark? Was he calling Denmark or someone in Russia, I wondered. His every move made me more and more suspicious. He did not seem like a student and he certainly didn't show much interest in what our delegation was doing.

Billy's back was turned toward me and I hoped to get close enough to hear what he was saying. If he was speaking in English I might find another piece to this puzzle. There was a large planter and decorative column next to the bank of three phones. A long dark red velvet drape hung alongside the column. A perfect place to hide while I listened, I thought. I slowly crept across the lobby, hugging the wall as much as I could. On past the newsstand, on past the easy chairs, I crept, and finally to the large drapes that hung from high above. Billy didn't notice me as he was still deeply involved in his conversation. Unfortunately, it was all in Russian but he was very polite to whomever he spoke. He shook his head up and down over and over while repeating the words "Da." "Da." "Da." It seemed as though someone was telling him what to do, or giving orders.

Finally, he said goodbye and slowly replaced the receiver in its cradle. He stared at the phone for a long time, apparently reflecting on what he was told. Then he headed across the lobby toward the elevator. I was well hidden and waited a long time until I was sure that it was safe to unravel myself from the folds in the drape.

After I left my self-contrived cocoon, I headed to the newsstand for a couple candy bars, then across the empty lobby toward the elevator. Once the elevator opened on my floor, the old Floor Lady recognized me and casually waved me past. No need for keys since Mike and Billy were already in the room.

As I pushed the door shut behind me, Mike and Billy looked up from their beds where they stretched out reading brochures and flyers they had picked up during the day. I tossed a candy bar on Mike's bed and told him that it was my treat. Billy looked at me with an inquisitive look, not quite figuring me out. Not friendly and actually not unfriendly. Perhaps he was a little suspicious of me, just as I was suspicious of him.

Chapter Nine

The Army Camp

Partly cloudy skies and cool breezes greeted our delegation, as we rode down long boulevards weaving through busy city traffic in the early morning. Still tired from yesterday's visit to Gorky Park, the students sat and quietly chatted. Others listened to their portable CD players or enjoyed the passing cityscape.

Erin and a girlfriend sat halfway down the aisle, while I joined Mike near the chaperones at the front. Billy found a seat by himself and stared at the small paper that he had got at the circus. He read it over and over again, almost as if he was memorizing it.

Mr. Reilly announced that we would first visit the Deputy Mayor of Moscow. He wanted to present him with a Letter of Greetings he had obtained from his State Senator at the Statehouse in Boston. This would be a formal presentation, he said, and everyone should be on his or her best behavior. Soon the bus pulled to a stop outside a large official-looking building. As the doors swung open, a man dressed in a policeman's uniform climbed aboard and spoke with Serge about protocol and where the students should be taken. Serge then translated for Mr. Reilly and the students. After a short wait, we filed quietly from the bus and followed Serge up a long staircase, onto a spacious marble landing. Just past the security checkpoints, we entered an official chamber filled with many desks positioned in a semicircle. At the open end was a single desk flanked by the Russian flag and a city flag.

Billy remained at the rear of our group while Erin worked her way forward and soon was at my side.

"Hi, Jimmy. Isn't this awesome?" she whispered.

"Yuh. How come Billy's just standing back there by the door and not up here with everybody?" I asked.

"I don't know. He's been acting somewhat cool today. Maybe it's just a bad day for him," she replied.

"Oh well, he probably ate something that didn't agree with him," I added, while not volunteering any of my real suspicions.

"Yuh. Hey, here comes someone," I whispered.

Just then the doors at the far end of the room opened wide. An old, officious heavy-set man quickly entered the room with a broad smile saying, "Welcome, Welcome, Americans." He spoke some English and then motioned the students to sit down at the many desks around the room. We were quite ready to accept his offer and scurried about filling the empty seats.

The mayor enthusiastically shook hands with our leaders. Then Serge stepped forward to explain in both Russian and English, the purpose of our visit to Moscow. He said that we were serving as student ambassadors from the United States and that we hoped to foster better relations with the Russians through direct contact with the everyday people. Serge then signaled Mr. Reilly to step forward.

Mr. Reilly extended the best wishes of the American people and presented the Deputy Mayor with a scrolled certificate of greetings from the Massachusetts Legislature. After shaking hands, the Deputy Mayor proudly accepted the gift along with two small flags from one of the students, one flag of the United States and one from Massachusetts.

Reaching down, he opened a side drawer in the center desk withdrawing a plastic bag. He carefully opened it and pulled out a large flag of Russia which he presented to Mr. Reilly. He also had many small flags for each student in the delegation and then offered the students cold bottles of cola and water. His assistant passed out cookies, as the Deputy Mayor circulated among the students shaking their hands. With the formal part of our visit concluded, we returned to the bus.

"Nicely done, everyone. I think the Deputy Mayor was impressed with you. Now, we're off to an Army camp. Again, be on your best behavior just like in the City Hall," Mr. Reilly cautioned.

The ride to the Army camp took us through the inner city, passing through some suburbs, and along a deserted stretch of highway. Eventually, we passed a grove of trees, turning left, and onto a military installation. Serge told us the large sign at the entrance stated this was a tank unit of nearly battalion size.

During our tour, we visited the soldiers' classrooms, barracks, and sports center. We also visited a large pool and gymnasium which were under renovation. We were encouraged to talk with, and question, any soldiers that we met. Many students offered to buy the pins and insignia that adorned the soldiers' uniforms. The soldiers, who apparently earned meager wages, were only too happy to sell them. They knew they could claim them as lost and be issued new ones. One soldier even freely gave his cap when a student only pointed at the insignia above its visor. The youthful soldiers seemed quite impressed with the females within our group and spent much time talking with them.

The highlight of our tour was the combat exercise involving about twenty soldiers on the athletic field. As we sat in the bleachers, the combat team mounted moving vehicles, fought off 'attackers', and demonstrated hand-to-hand combat and karate. One-on-one socializing followed, and some students even had an opportunity to fire AK-47 assault rifles. From the athletic field we moved to a tank display to learn of their capabilities from an English-speaking soldier.

Eventually we headed back to the city in the late afternoon. Everyone was thrilled with the unexpected souvenirs that they had accumulated at the Army camp, and the girls chatted endlessly about the handsome young soldiers they had met.

As we passed small villages and farmlands, I heard Mr. Reilly tell Serge "Too late for dinner at the hotel." Then he whispered something else to him. Serge translated for the driver. This, I later realized was a request to make an unscheduled stop in Moscow.

To the delight of all, we again found ourselves stopping at the Arbat Street McDonald's where we happily dined on American favorites.

Erin and I enjoyed our meal and talked about the day's activities, while Billy made another telephone call and then seemed to just disappear. I felt comfortable that I was again making some headway with Erin and was also thankful that Billy wasn't around. I had watched him all day and found nothing suspicious about his activity. Maybe his secretive meetings were meaningless, a result of my over-zealous imagination, I thought. Nevertheless, I would continue to watch him, as I still knew he was up to something. I couldn't put my finger on it, but was sure that he was involved in something sinister.

Erin was completely oblivious about what I knew, and I thought it best to keep it that way for the time being.

After we finished eating, Mr. Reilly raised his cap and called out, "Follow me."

He led our parade of students on a walking tour past many stores with well-decorated windows and couples enjoying an early evening stroll. Small groups of teen-agers loitered on street corners. Eventually, we arrived at a nearby Metro station.

Stopping at the entrance, he announced, "The ladies and I would like to treat you all to a Metro ride back to our hotel. That is, if you want to come."

The excited students happily agreed and jumped at the opportunity to ride Moscow's famous subway system, the Metro. We thanked the chaperones repeatedly, as we scampered down the long flight of stairs toward the rumbling sounds below.

It was shortly after seven-thirty when we arrived back at the hotel. We had hoped for some free time, yet Mrs. Renaud gathered us together outside the hotel.

"May I have your attention, please?" she asked.

After she waited a few moments, the chatter finally subsided and she continued.

"It's too early for bed," she said. "I think it would be beneficial to take a moment to share some of our thoughts. Therefore, I'd like everyone to meet outside the Game Room and sit in a large circle on the floor for a few minutes."

She loved games and asked each person to name one positive thing that they learned on this trip. Erin sat beside me and when it came to her turn she mentioned some historical fact, like so many of the others. I couldn't help saying that I learned what true friendship meant and that some people don't realize that others offer friendship in different ways. Erin quickly turned her head towards me as she felt that the statement somehow related to her.

"Very nice thought, Jimmy. Thank you," Mrs. Renaud commented.

After the activity, Erin continued to glance at me with a puzzled look as if she were still trying to interpret my comment. Maybe this was the signal that she needed.

"Okay, everyone, you are free to do as you wish as long as you stay in the hotel. Remember that bed check will be at eleven. I suggest that you get busy with your journals. Our week in Moscow will be over soon," Mrs. Renaud reminded us.

*****

A jangling telephone jolted me out of bed as the early morning sun streamed through the window blinds. Squinting at my watch I confirmed that this was our 'wake-up call.' Billy was first into the shower, while Mike brushed his teeth in the bathroom. I took the opportunity to pull the crumpled piece of paper from Billy's pants' pocket. An address and a sketchy map were scribbled on it. This must be where he'll meet someone, I thought, and then I quickly put the paper back.

We walked past the elevator, deciding to take the stairs instead. We thought the exercise would do us some good. Four flights later we reached the lobby. The door which opened into the dining room was located just off the lobby. During breakfast, Mr. Reilly announced to everyone that today we would visit Camp Zemchusina along the Moscow River. He said that this had been an old Soviet Youth Camp where the best of the promising young students spent a summer holiday. There, the students were immersed in sports activities and propaganda sessions that expounded the glories of Communism. With the fall of Communism, however, the camp's budget was drastically cut, and it was then opened to any group wishing to book a one- or two-week stay. Beds and meals were provided, but that was all. Any other activities were at the discretion of the visitors' organizer.

On our way to Camp Zemchusina, we briefly stopped at Red Square, but this time to have a group photo taken in front of St. Basil's Cathedral. A professional photographer waited for our group and quickly arranged everyone, tallest to the rear, shortest in front. Mrs. Kolinsky said that the photos would be delivered to our hotel the next morning.

Camp Zemchusina was located approximately thirty miles from Moscow, nestled in the woodlands along the quiet, meandering Moscow River. We arrived shortly before noon and were welcomed by a young Russian girl in traditional costume. She offered us salted bread, as was the custom, and then invited us into a communal dining room. After lunch, we met with a Russian student delegation from Novgorod (northwest of Moscow). The Camp Director asked Serge to invite our delegation to sing some typical American songs. He told Mrs. Renaud who happily led our group in singing a few traditional and popular songs while our counterparts offered us their favorite musical numbers. We then exchanged token gifts, and shared our small albums filled with photographs of our hometowns and families. Erin and I especially enjoyed learning how to pronounce and write, in Russian, our names and expressions of politeness.

I saw Billy speak briefly with Mr. Reilly before he wandered over to Erin and me.

"Sorry guys, but I won't be able to hang out with you today. Got somethin' to take care of."

"What's up, Billy? Need any help?" I asked.

"Not really. My aunt is sick and I need to call to find out if she'll be okay. Don't worry. I'll be back later. Mr. Reilly said it was okay."

I didn't believe his unlikely story. He was still involved with something. I just knew it. Mr. Reilly would never let anyone just disappear from the group. Erin didn't give it much thought but Billy's disappearance only added to my suspicions about his strange, unexplained activities.

Later in the afternoon, our group went for row boat rides on the river and picked wild berries in the surrounding fields. Walking tours to an adjoining village brought us past, small dachas (country homes), and hard-working peasants toiling in the nearby fields, all of which added to a feeling of peacefulness and serenity.

After dinner, Mrs. Renaud asked us to head over to the camp gym for a special presentation. There we found a troupe of Russian folk dancers dressed in traditional ethnic costumes. They danced and sang for our entertainment. Some men provided a musical accompaniment and even played a few solos on strange stringed instruments called 'balalaikas.'

The dancers were insistent that the American delegation join in. Our chaperones were the first to amuse us with their frail attempts to dance Russian-style. Not to be outdone, the rest of the students finally joined with the happy twirling dancers. Erin and I became partners moving about to the fast-paced music. The dances were somewhat like our square dances. Everyone laughed as we missed our steps and paraded out of sequence to new partners across the floor. The chaperones seemed to make the most mistakes, and we laughed at their vain attempts to perform the dance seriously. There was a sigh of relief, however, when the dance finally ended. After we caught our breaths, the next dance began.

Eventually, Erin and I plopped ourselves down and laughed as we talked about the chaperones awkward attempts to dance Russian style. We also reflected on the soldiers and others that we had met and how Russia wasn't as scary as we had once thought.

The ride back to the Metropole was again quiet as we rolled down the darkened roadways that led back through the urban maze. The hum of the tires seemed to lull many students to sleep. Passing plowed fields and small villages, I could only gaze at the blur outside and think of all that I had seen and witnessed. I had learned much about Russia, and now felt much more comfortable traveling and meeting people. Erin and I were also beginning to share a common bond. I began to feel more comfortable about trusting her and even toyed with the thought of letting her in on my suspicions about Billy. Maybe she could shed some light on his behavior and how his actions weren't in keeping with the goals of our group. I decided to put off any discussion a while longer and again turned to the window to watch the passing blur.

Chapter Ten

Zwenigorod and Khubinkah

Mrs. Kolinsky energetically carried out the honors today of counting heads, as I sorted through my day-bag searching for extra film.

"Thirty six, and thirty seven," she whispered as she completed her count.

She then nodded to Mr. Reilly who, in turn, signaled the driver that we were all accounted for.

This seemed strange since Billy was not on the bus. I informed Mrs. Kolinsky and Mr. Reilly. They didn't seem to be too bothered, however, and signaled the driver to start the bus anyway. After thanking me for my alertness, Mr. Reilly whispered something to the two women, as they settled back and chatted quietly, obviously not bothered by Billy's absence. I wondered if anyone else was aware of Billy's freedom to come and go as he wished. Apparently, he had already cleared with Mr. Reilly. I was now convinced that something was 'fishy' and I would have to try even harder to find out about Billy if he ever returned to our group.

About forty-five miles east of Moscow lay the town of Zwenigorod, the "Town of Bells." Billy met us there but kept his distance from Erin and me. This seemed strange, but I still hesitated to get Erin involved with my concerns. His disappearance hadn't lasted long and I wondered how he had caught up with us so soon. For an American living in Denmark, he sure knew his way around Russian cities.

Zwenigorod was home to a large, sprawling monastery and cathedral which was under renovation. Sections were still open to visitors, however. The deteriorated complex easily filled four acres. Old stucco-covered fieldstone walls were partially whitewashed. Flakes of fallen paint revealed the mortared stones beneath. A shady, dirt path led to a small museum which housed many old chalices and relics formerly used by the monks. These stood as reminders of the days when religious faith played a major roll within the villages.

The small town of Zwenigorod grew nearby in the shadow of the old onion-domed monastery. A few shops lined the streets. Erin and I peered into the shop windows, as we strolled along, and visited the small markets where older peasants sat on wooden crates, waiting patiently to sell their meager assortment of home-grown potatoes and vegetables. Old automotive relics, still operational, were parked along the curbside and drew our curiosity, as we continued exploring the small town. There were many photo opportunities and a number of students made good use of them.

Old woman peddles home-grown vegetables.

At a street corner, an ice cream peddler sold small paper cups filled with ice cream for only 100 rubles (10 cents). This quickly became a favorite stopping point for many students in the group. As the temperature steadily climbed under the hot summer sun, this enterprising merchant enjoyed a handsome profit from all the sales he made this morning. I waited in line while the old man reached deeply into the ice cream chest and scooped out his ice cold treasures. I bought Erin and myself a cup of citron-flavored ice cream. We ate it with small wooden spoons, as we strolled across the main street and into a small park. A solitary park bench under a large chestnut tree offered us a shady respite from which to escape the heat of a noontime sun.

"You never did tell me what college you were going to next September, Jimmy," Erin inquired.

"Oh, I didn't? Sorry. Well, I applied to a few but finally settled on Northeastern University. I plan to take financial management courses. My dad has connections in New York and said that he could get me set up."

"Is this what you really want to do?"

"Well, not exactly. I've always wanted to join the Army as an officer and really see the world. Northeastern has an Army ROTC program and I was thinking about signing up for it. Maybe I could do both. What d'ya think?"

"Oh, of course, I think it would be super. I even thought of joining up too, but I think I would be too chicken to follow through. Anyway, my dad says that's men's work. I know that they are pushing me to study harder so that I'll get into some college and become a big success."

"Well, some jobs might be better for a man but there are many for women too. If you don't join up, what would you like to do, Erin?"

"Well, I thought maybe I'd look into teaching in some public school, somewhere, maybe in Haverhill, Newburyport, or Amesbury. I know the salary isn't too good but I'd really like to work with children. You know, I have a cousin, Heather, who is a teacher in New Jersey and she makes a really good salary. Maybe I should work down there. She teaches middle school, seventh grade science, and loves it."

"Say, if you worked in New Jersey and I worked in New York, maybe we could see each other sometime. Wouldn't that be neat," I mused.

"Yuh, it'd be really somethin'," Erin said laughingly. "Actually, I wouldn't care about the money so much. I like kids and teaching them would be sort of fun and a real challenge too."

"Boy, you're right about that. You must have loads of patience to be a teacher, but I suppose it could be fun too," I replied.

I felt a sense of confidence and safety in opening up to Erin. She wasn't like other girls that I had met. Oh, she had her moments though. She was both dependent and independent, neither judgmental nor condescending. She was always positive and accepting and seemed to exude a self-confidence and self-direction that showed quite a bit of maturity. She was so easy to talk to, and I was beginning to like her more each day.

"Well, I guess we'd better go," I said, although wanting to linger a while longer.

We strolled slowly along the cobbled stone sidewalk, stopping a moment while Erin picked some wildflowers from a nearby grassy field. Our bus was waiting in the motor park directly ahead.

"You know, Jimmy, I really like this town. It seems so peaceful here. The people are friendly and polite too. You don't find much of that back home. Everyone there is in such a rush to go no where. Do you think we'll ever get a chance to visit here again?" she asked, although knowing the answer to the question already.

"Maybe, but I wouldn't count on it," I replied.

A short distance ahead, in the motor park, we saw Mr. Reilly talking to Serge and our bus driver. As we reached the bus Mr. Reilly greeted us with a pleasant hello. This was unusual as he seldom offered such pleasantries.

"Hi Erin, Jimmy. Having a good time?" he asked.

"Yup, this is great," Erin replied.

"Yuh, this has been a super trip. Thanks for having us along, Mr. Reilly," I joined in.

After a short wait, we were again cruising along the highway. Next stop was at an Air Military Unit (air base) in the town of Khubinkah. Serge said that it was a military airfield nearly 25 minutes from Zwenigorod. Its mission was the defense of Moscow, and it was home to Russia's 'Top Guns'. Through the trees, along the base's main road, we saw six MIG 29's standing in rows along the tarmac while mechanics serviced them.

A retired Air Force Major who said he had flown MIG 15's and 17's in earlier days led us through the Air Museum. About six or seven static displays filled each room. Our tour guide, Major

Raskin, led us from room to room, proudly explaining each item and adding interesting tidbits about his connection with the displays. Upon leaving the old museum building, we found ourselves facing many old, vintage jet fighters that had been hollowed-out. The students eagerly climbed into the cockpits or posed for pictures with the Major. A short while later, Major Raskin opened a small kiosk for the souvenir-hungry students who quickly scooped up pins and jet fighter calendars.

After again boarding our busses, we retraced our journey along the long winding country roads toward Moscow. Unexpectedly, our coach slowed as we approached Camp Zemchusina which was on the highway leading back to Moscow. Our driver turned, and we headed through the arched gates. Mr. Reilly picked up the microphone and announced that we had some extra time today so he planned a 'back to nature' three-kilometer walk upstream along the Moscow River.

"Good exercise and fresh air," Mr. Reilly told us. "Besides, we'll visit a small village and hopefully, talk with some natives."

A number of groans were heard from the rear of the coach from some students who were more content to sit in their comfortable seats and observe Russian villages from afar.

Passing by large fields filled with summer wildflowers and crossing over small shallow streams, we followed a worn path which eventually brought us to the village of Ryazm (population:

257). As we strolled down the main street, under a warm mid-afternoon sun, we clicked away with our cameras. Old people, children, small dachas, and animals were ours to capture on film. An interesting, though out of place, two-story, red-bricked house caught our attention. It was being built in stark contrast to the neighboring, single story, log homes.

Our guide, Serge, was also curious, so he strolled over to a heavy set woman tending a small garden. He returned after a few minutes to share with the delegation all that he learned.

"She told me that a 30-year old Moscow contractor was building the house. She also said that we could look inside since the workers had gone home for the day," he said, and then continued on.

"The daily gossip within the village was that neither the contractor nor his house was welcomed in Ryazm. Most villagers thought that the contractor was one of many despised Moscow bureaucrats. They were party loyalists who had no scruples and lived off the hard labors of the common people, skimming money for themselves. The local gentry apparently had use for neither the government nor those who worked for it."

"Between the new house and the wide Moscow River out back, was a large garden already planted with assorted vegetables. A two-car garage and large, interior rooms with central heat were luxuries of which the villagers could only dream," Serge said.

As dusk settled in, we walked back to Camp Zemchusina, just as the large red sun slid behind a cluster of towering evergreen trees. The visit to Ryazm was very interesting and quite enlightening.

The camp had arranged to have a bonfire for some other guests and invited us to join in. With the early evening arrival of mosquitoes, everyone gathered closely to the fire while throwing small wooden sticks and old papers onto the burning logs as added fuel. Larger logs had been rolled close to the roaring fire and provided seating for the small crowd of Russians and Americans who joyfully chatted and intermingled. Billy, who had been gone the whole day, arrived and worked his way through the crowd. Apparently happy to see familiar faces, he decided to join Erin and me. We squeezed together to allow enough space for him to sit. He told us about a meeting he had with the camp director and said that they talked about the history of the camp; a story that I didn't believe. He said nothing about that sick aunt that he was so concerned about earlier in the day. Erin and I let him ramble on while enjoying the warmth of the fire.

Soon some Russian students started to sing and were quickly joined by the others. They continued with additional songs, to the delight and appreciation of their new foreign friends. The beautiful music filled the air and seemed to add a warm sense of serenity as the fire crackled amidst glowing red embers. Elisabeth and Monika were outgoing girls. Not to be outdone, they jumped at the opportunity to lead the American students singing 'The Brady Bunch' and 'America, the Beautiful.' We quickly joined them singing loudly, while Billy chose only to sit and listen quietly.

The fire slowly died, and a warm glow was all that remained. Mosquitoes again reclaimed their territory as many students pulled their jackets over their heads in a vain attempt to stem the advance of the unwelcome attackers. The once jubilant Russian entourage quickly slipped away toward their camp dormitories after bidding us farewell. We slowly returned to our bus, waiting near the camp entrance. After our usual headcount, we rolled along into the darkness toward the illuminated skies over Moscow. Our delegation seemed quite pleased with all that we had done on this trip, and few looked forward to returning to the States. Tomorrow was going to be our free day, and I heard some students eagerly planning their activities as our bus continued down the highway. I did not mention anything to Erin about our free day, as I was torn between telling her about Billy's activities and finding answers for myself.

The darkened roadways evolved into wider boulevards where taxis and motorists zipped along in the late evening traffic. The Metropole stood apart from the other buildings, with an awning-covered entrance and large, brightly lit lobby. Two security guards dutifully stood on either side of the doorway. They again welcomed us back, while keeping a watchful eye for any unsavory characters lingering about.

    We climbed the steps to the lobby as one of the guards opened the door for our group. We smiled and nodded to acknowledge his kind gesture. As we passed through the lobby, the manager ran toward Serge saying, in Russian, that the elevator was broken but would be fixed later that night. He was obviously very sorry. Serge then passed the bad news on to everyone. A number of groans could be heard as no one relished the thought of climbing four or five flights of stairs. Reluctantly, everyone headed for the stairwell and dragged themselves up the many stairs to the waiting Floor Ladies.

Chapter Eleven

Gumshoes

Today was to be our free day in Moscow. The students had looked forward to it all week. Armed with rubles, subway maps, lists of attractions, and courage, many students quickly set out while some opted to stay in small groups for reasons of security or economy. Mr. Reilly advised us to always stay in mixed groups of at least two people. He also provided us with the name, address, and telephone number of the hotel and his own cell phone number. Everyone was excited about their 'day of freedom' in Moscow and had hurried to the dining room, gulped down their meals, and scattered in every direction.

I searched for Erin as I entered the dining room. I knew that I needed to confide in someone. Perhaps she might be able to shed some light on Billy's strange behavior. There she was, alone, in the corner and I quickly headed toward her, bypassing the buffet table. Billy's actions and my suspicions were soon 'on the table.' The trail of evidence I already had about the street peddler and the circus incident slowly began to sink in, catching her quite by surprise. She sat there in disbelief, shaking her head slowly from side to side.

"I don't believe this. I just don't believe this," she uttered. "If you thought Billy was mixed up in something, why didn't you go to Mr. Reilly right away?"

"I don't know. He wouldn't have believed me anyway. Billy and I have had our ups and downs, but I don't want him getting into any serious trouble. I have to follow him today, Erin, and find out what he's up to. I just have to. I can't do it alone. I need your help," I pleaded. "Erin, you gotta help me. I don't know what he's into, but I'm sure he's in over his head."

"Okay, okay. Calm down, Jimmy."

"What do you think he's up to?" I asked her.

"It's probably nothing at all. Jimmy, I think you're really too suspicious and over-reacting. I know that you don't really like Billy," Erin replied.

"What do you mean by that? Like I said, we've had some disagreements, but whether I like him or not has nothing to do with what I'm tellin' you."

"Oh really, I've noticed the way you looked at him on the bus," she went on. "You aren't very good at hiding your feelings about him, you know."

"Oh, come on. I just think he's into something serious, that's all. I like him as well as anyone, but I don't feel right about what's he's up to."

"Oh, Jimmy, lighten up. He probably has some friends here and wanted to see them again," Erin rationalized.

"What? Friends? In the middle of the night? And behind circus wagons? Oh, come on, Erin, you know that doesn't make any sense."

"So, I suppose, he's some kind of gangster, huh?" she said with apparent skepticism.

"No, um, I mean, maybe. I don't know."

"What can we do?" she asked, "Maybe we should just tell Mr. Reilly. He'll know what to do."

"No. All I've got are my suspicions and the fact that I saw Billy meet some Russians. That wouldn't raise any red flags with Mr. Reilly. We've got to have something more solid. I mean, I think we should follow Billy today and maybe we'll learn more. I could sure use some help. Are you with me?"

"Of course I am," she said, with an air of excitement in her voice. "But you're gonna find out just how wrong you are."

"We'll see. Remember, not a word to anyone else," I admonished.

"You know me. We'd better find Billy before he leaves the hotel," she said as we stood up from the table.

We left the dining room and spotted Billy by the newsstand in the nearly deserted lobby. The other students had already wandered in all directions. As a large wall clock struck nine, I saw Billy pick up a newspaper and hand the hotel vendor his money. He briefly glanced at his watch, and quickly left the hotel. We followed him at a safe distance out into the busy street.

Billy flagged a taxi and said something to the driver as he crawled in. Contrary to Mr. Reilly's instructions, Billy was traveling alone. He handed the driver a small piece of paper with the address, and the taxi then sped off. Erin and I waved down another taxi and told the driver to follow Billy's taxi. Luckily, the driver understood some English and was quick to comply. Erin and I were now committed to solving this puzzle. I was glad that she was there with me as it gave me the courage to follow this mystery through.

We whizzed by many small boutiques, American franchises, and past Moscow University. The city streets were busy with people who scurried to work and shoppers seeking early morning bargains. A cloud of carbon monoxide haze filled the city canyons and added to the overall dreary scene. Small crowds gathered at every street corner and waited patiently for the 'Walk' signal before continuing through the urban maze.

Billy's taxi then pulled into a small side street and stopped next to a four-story red brick apartment building. Our driver stopped just past this street. I must have overpaid our fare, as the driver thanked us repeatedly with a broad smile. Erin and I quickly jumped from the cab and raced around the corner just in time to see Billy climb a narrow set of stairs leading to a worn brown entry way. To the side was an array of doorbells and nameplates. He hesitated a moment, then pushed one of the upper bells. A buzzer unlocked the door and he slowly entered. It slammed shut behind him, and we were locked out.

We darted from the corner, where we were hiding, crossed the street, and scrambled up the stairs to the entryway. Facing the same row of bells marking the occupants' names in faded Cyrillic letters, I turned to Erin, not knowing which button to push.

"We can't get in, Erin, unless someone inside pushes their buzzer. Which one do I push?" I asked.

"Push one of the bottom buttons," Erin urged. "At least we will be able to get in. If you push a top one, it might be the apartment where Billy is and he'll know that we followed him here."

I did as she suggested and a loud buzz unlocked the door. Once inside, an old woman on the first floor opened her door and apparently asked what we wanted. We could only reply by shrugging our shoulders. She shook her head with disgust and returned to her apartment, apparently unimpressed by our rudeness. We then ran to each upper floor to find Billy.

Erin and I listened at each door, hoping to hear his voice. She took the left side while I took the right side. Halfway down the hallway, our search abruptly ended.

"He's in here," Erin whispered.

From the keyhole I could see Billy sitting in a big overstuffed chair while a well-dressed man sat opposite him. A second man stood next to the stuffed chair. He said nothing but quietly stared at Billy. I was sure that he must have been a guard as he hovered over the one seated. A bodyguard, I thought. The room was dimly lit, yet bright enough to easily distinguish its occupants.

"You ain't nothin' but a kid," the older man said in his broken English.

"Yuh, but I've got good connections in da States. No need to worry," Billy assured him. "I'll have the money when you have the stuff."

"You better or you're dead, kid," he shot back.

"What's going on?" Erin inquired.

"Shhh, I can't hear," I whispered.

While trying to hide his fear, Billy apparently wanted to confirm a later rendezvous and leave.

"Okay, when and where?" he asked.

"What's the hurry?" the dark figure asked while sitting back in his chair.

Billy responded "I can't be away from my group much more. My delegation leader will become suspicious and stop me. I'm already taking a big chance, so let's get this over with."

"Okay. This afternoon, at four, Red Square. Bus 14. That okay with you?" he asked.

"Yuh!" Billy said as he stood up.

"Remember," the stranger admonished as he wagged his finger, "any tricks and you're dead."

"Quick, let's get out of here," I blurted out to Erin while nearly pushing her aside.

We raced to the stairs and were nearly at the bottom when I heard the apartment door slam shut above us. Outside, Erin and I hid behind a nearby trash dumpster until Billy emerged alone from the old brick apartment building. He walked at a quick, nervous pace to the busy corner intersection. We scurried from our hiding place seeking cover behind every barrel, tree, and staircase along the way. He turned the corner and melted into a sea of pedestrians, nearly becoming lost on the crowded sidewalks. Erin, now caught up in this mystery, made sure that she didn't lose sight of Billy. As we followed, I brought Erin up to speed on what I had seen and heard at the apartment. She was stunned and thought, for sure, that Billy must be into something serious.

After we tailed him for nearly a half hour, Billy arrived at a Militia (Police) building. He suddenly stopped and turned around, as if he were suspicious that someone might be following him. He didn't see Erin or me. We were mixed in with a large group of people across the street waiting for a traffic signal to change. Apparently feeling that he was safe, he disappeared into the Militia doorway. We felt it better to wait a safe distance away and to sort out this strange turn of events. A store entry offered us what we needed, a good concealed vantage point.

"If he's into something illegal, why is he going to the police? After all, he just made some sort of deal with the man back at the apartment building. Maybe he wants to buy something, guns, drugs, information, or whatever," Erin puzzled. "Maybe we should call Mr. Reilly now before anything serious happens," Erin begged.

"Yuh, I think you're right. We're getting in over our heads," I finally admitted.

Erin's frantic call to Mr. Reilly

Nearby on the sidewalk was a public telephone and, with luck, I had the correct number of kopeks. Erin grabbed the phone first and tried to call Mr. Reilly. She knew that he would not be at the hotel so she called his cell telephone number as he suggested. To her surprise, an international telephone operator came on the line and said that cell phone numbers were not yet operational in Russia.

"Darn," she bellowed and slammed the receiver back into its cradle. "We're on our own, Jimmy. Mr. Reilly's cell phone doesn't work in Russia and we have no way to contact him."

"Maybe Mrs. Renaud or Mrs. Kolinsky will be at the hotel, Erin. Shouldn't we try to call them?"

"Ain't no use, I heard them tell Mr. Reilly that they were going out together shopping at the GUM store at Red Square. It's only a few blocks away. If we're lucky, maybe we'll see them if we go to Red Square," she added, with some skepticism.

"Yuh. Hey, look Erin. There's Billy coming out of the police station."

Billy was carrying a small black briefcase, which he must have gotten in the police station. He appeared more relaxed and confident as he strolled down the wide avenue toward a small park filled with many women pushing baby strollers. A refreshing, westerly breeze tempered the warm noontime sun as Billy found an empty bench upon which to rest. He opened the briefcase as if to reassure himself of its contents. Once satisfied, he snapped it shut. He pulled the rumpled newspaper which he had bought at the hotel out of his back pocket. Carefully folding the pages, he began to read it while waiting for his four o'clock rendezvous in Red Square.

Erin and I sat across the park from Billy and exchanged our thoughts and feelings about the trip and this mystery in which we now found ourselves involved. We tried to figure out Billy's actions and knew that we certainly had to tell Mr. Reilly. If only his cell phone worked here, I thought. No matter, Erin and I would be able to handle whatever came up. At least we thought so.

A sausage, roll, and soda from one of the many vendors in the park helped us pass the time while Billy continued reading his newspaper.

Before long, another street peddler strolled our way and surmised that we were Americans, or at least foreigners, and approached Erin. A persistent man with an array of matrioska (nesting) dolls. He wore baggy pants, a dirty shirt, and had a three-day growth of beard, which partially hid his pockmarked face. He spoke relatively good English and willingly lowered his asking price each time we told him that we weren't interested. Since he was becoming a distraction and might blow our cover with his boastful sales pitch, I bought one doll for Erin. For this, he was eternally grateful and left us alone.

The chatter of small children playing nearby reminded me of our visit to Gorky Park. There were so many happy faces as young boys played with marbles, and the girls studied their strategy or wandered off to the swings. Mothers apparently exchanged gossip while they rocked their strollers laden with precious cargo. Tall, lush trees provided a comforting shelter from the noontime heat. Nearby a small wading pool served as a gathering place for some children who had model sailboats that they wished to sail. A few parents sat by the pool fanning air into the sails in hopes to move the small boats more quickly away from 'shore'. An old woman sat a few feet away, feeding small bits of bread to a group of pigeons who eagerly scooped up each morsel. Three or four older children rode their bicycles along the pathway, dodging older pensioners and smaller children. This 'American turn-of-the-century' scene seemed to offer a surreal tranquility that belied the events that were soon to follow.

By mid-afternoon, Billy threw his newspaper in a trash barrel and headed for the street. He hailed a taxi and was soon out of sight. I hoped he was heading to Red Square as we ran to catch another taxi and follow him. We found an empty taxi at the corner and told the driver to take us to Lenin's Mausoleum in Red Square. Unfortunately, he spoke no English. Failing in our attempts to explain our destination, Erin reached in her purse and pulled out a small travel brochure.

"Here, Jimmy, show him this picture."

The brochure's cover featured a full color picture of the mausoleum. When I shoved the brochure toward the driver, he smiled and shook his head to indicate that he understood. He shifted gears and sped off, along the wide congested streets.

Even though Billy was now out of sight, we knew that we were not far behind him. Luckily, our driver seemed to know some shortcuts as we arrived in Red Square just as Billy's taxi pulled to a stop ahead of us. After settling our fare with the taxi driver, we saw Billy walking directly toward Saint Basil's Cathedral across the open square. In front of the cathedral sat rows of parked tour buses and three burly figures that stood in the dark recess between two of the buses.

The happy sounds of innocent children at play now seemed so remote, as Erin and I watched Billy from a distance. He strolled slowly toward the cluster of busses parked near St. Basil's Cathedral.

Chapter Twelve

The Exchange

An island within a metropolis, Red Square was lined with cobblestones, and mostly devoid of any vegetation. Gathering clouds cast a gray pall over the last remaining tour busses opposite the mausoleum. An eerie silence prevailed as a few lonely tourists crossed the square's wide expanse in the late afternoon.

Red Square was long known for annual May Day Parades, when the Soviet Union would display before the eyes of the world every conceivable form or armored vehicle, weaponry, and ballistic missile. Communist leaders and Politburo dignitaries would stand proudly above Lenin's Tomb to salute their military forces as crowds cheered the grand arsenal of Soviet military power. Certainly, it was a real propaganda ploy to project the influence of a bankrupt empire. Now, the square is essentially deserted, a moot reminder of past glory days. Tourists and pigeons lay claim to this vast expanse of historical real estate.

The Kremlin Wall

On this warm afternoon, a few Muscovites and some foreign tourists visited the graves of former leaders, along with citizens who longed for the security of past decades. Many visitors stopped to snap photographs. Red Square was a magnet for locals and tourists alike.

Along the famed Kremlin Wall, former dictators are buried. Their graves have been marked with busts of their likenesses. The images seemed to bear silent witness to the follies of Communism. Lenin's Tomb stands alone like a sentry of the old guard, still protected by young Russian military honor guards.

On the opposite side of the square was the beautiful St. Basil's Cathedral. Skilled designers and craftsmen created the ornate cathedral with its many onion-shaped, spiraled domes painted in soft colors. Around the house of worship, many smaller statues of saints were carved. The cathedral's inspiring beauty captivates many tourists. Facing both the Tomb of Lenin and the St. Basil's is the famous GUM department store with its array of fancy, imported merchandise affordable only to the very wealthy. Similar to an indoor multistory mall, many small kiosks lined each side of the mezzanine. A glass dome graced its central roofline.

I could but wonder about the triangle's symbolism. Here we find the decaying godless Communism (Lenin's Tomb), the materialism of western capitalism (GUM department store), and the overriding eternal power of God (St. Basil's Cathedral). Could it be that no one else recognized these three powerful forces of the 20th Century clustered so closely together? I briefly reflected on this unusual trilogy of ideology and the power struggles that involved these three forces.

The queue to visit Lenin's Tomb snaked back and forth as many people quietly waited their turn in the air-conditioned mausoleum. The square was otherwise deserted.

Billy seemed nervous as he plodded along. Pausing, he glanced over his shoulder, apparently wondering if he were being followed. Erin and I followed at a safe distance, hidden by a street vendor selling sausages and cold drinks. I saw Billy stop for a moment and fumble with the crumpled paper that he removed from his pocket. He slowly panned the parked coaches before him. He proceeded cautiously toward the parked busses clustered tightly in the corner of the square. Three dark figures stood by one bus, and then disappeared into the shadows. Billy checked numbers on each coach as he worked his way through the maze. Finally he stopped in front of a large, green Mercedes coach with the number 14 painted neatly on the side.

Some busses were unattended while the drivers huddled together some distance away, smoking cigarettes and exchanging daily gossip. Other drivers sat patiently in their idling coaches while their passengers melted into the recesses of Red Square.

Bus 14, at first, appeared empty. Its narrow door had been left ajar. Slowly, Billy pushed the door open and climbed the steps. There, at the rear of the coach, were three men.

Erin and I slipped along the side of the busses, unnoticed by the men in Billy's bus. We climbed onto the adjacent bus and crawled down the long aisle to the back row. Curtains covered the rear windows yet allowed us enough of an opening to peek through.

From our position, Erin and I could see that one man was seated and two were standing. I had never seen the seated man before, yet I later learned that he was Mr. Kastrovna. Wearing a neat black suit and puffing on a big cigar, he motioned Billy closer while studying his every move. Billy slowly walked down the aisle checking seats on both sides for any hidden surprises. Two husky men stood across from Mr. Kastrovna with their jackets open, partially exposing shoulder weapons. I recognized one of them from the meeting at the apartment house earlier that day. Cigar smoke filled the rear of the bus and formed a nauseous haze.

From our location at the rear of the adjacent coach, we could see all that happened in Billy's bus. Erin was very nervous and wished that she was somewhere else, actually anywhere else, other than caught up in this intrigue. We remained motionless, safely hidden by the partially drawn curtains and saw much of what was happening. Unfortunately, we could not hear what any of them were saying. After their brief conversation, I saw the seated Russian unstrap and open his briefcase, which was filled with some white substances wrapped in plastic pouches. In turn, Billy also opened his briefcase. Neatly stacked in packs were many ruble banknotes banded together. The two men exchanged briefcases and then Billy left the bus followed by these three mobsters.

Once outside, I saw Billy run quickly around the front of our bus and scramble inside just as police converged from every direction. Flashing lights, deafening sirens, and screeching tires shattered the peacefulness of late afternoon. As they jumped from their cars, the police hollered orders of some type. Billy scurried under the first row of seats while we continued hiding in the rear.

Repeated demands from the police went unheeded. The three Russians appeared trapped between our coach and the one that they had just left. Not wishing to miss any part of this intense confrontation, I continued peering out of the window. Both of the Russian bodyguards drew their weapons and began firing at the police. Bullets ricocheted off the police cars; others smashed into the windows of our bus. With little room to maneuver, the Russian drug dealers sought shelter behind Bus 14.

Tourists who were heading back to their busses ran screaming for cover across the square to a narrow row of trees near the Kremlin Wall. Bus drivers, who previously gossiped in small gatherings away from the busses, also ran for safety with the tourists. I even saw guards at Lenin's tomb attentively watch from a distance. They apparently did not wish to get involved but did observe all that happened. They immediately ushered all visitors from the mausoleum and assumed new posts at the entrance door. Red Square was now essentially deserted. There was a silence broken only by the sounds of gunfire and unheeded demands to surrender.

Realizing that they were out-numbered, Mr. Kastrovna yelled orders to his two associates. They crowded close to him, perhaps to act as shields. All three maneuvered quickly around the rear of our coach. A hail of gunfire again broke the eerie silence and tranquility of the square. Bullets pierced the windshield and sides of our bus. Chards of glass flew through the air and littered the aisles. Erin and I held each other tightly and crouched closely to the floor. Billy continued to hide under seats near the front of the coach.

With all escape routes blocked, the three men scurried along the side of our bus and through the open door. Looking up the long aisle, I could see the first thug climb the steps toward the driver's seat. Just then a bullet struck him. He spun around, and fell down the steps and out onto the pavement. Mr. Kastrovna and the other bodyguard managed to climb over him. They scrambled through the open door and up the steps, using the bus for protection.

Mr. Kastrovna and his second bodyguard lay on the floor. They spoke for a few moments, discussing their plan of escape, I thought. The bodyguard then reached up, and pulled the idling bus into drive. It slowly rolled forward under heavy gunfire. They were too busy to notice me, so I peered out, through two sections of a curtain, to see what was happening. Erin was still curled tightly in the corner. The bus rolled on, barely missing the wounded bodyguard who lay on the bloody cobblestones below. Now gaining speed, we headed directly toward one of the police cars. The police, who initially used their vehicles for protection, now scurried in all directions. The large bus slammed into one patrol car, throwing it aside like a child's toy.

The bodyguard must have felt safe as he then climbed into the driver's seat, grabbed the steering wheel, and shifted into high speed. The bus roared out of Red Square belching dark plumes of exhaust.

Three police cars followed close behind. The bus thundered down Mindenkov Street, nearly hitting a taxi that crossed ahead of it. On-lookers turned to see this fast rolling motor chase through the busy late afternoon traffic.

Standing brazenly in the aisle, Mr. Kastrovna checked the windows on both sides. From under the seats, I could see Billy trying to remain motionless and quiet. He must have known that they'd kill him if they discovered him. Just then the bus made a sharp turn. Billy's briefcase slid from under his seat into the aisle. Mr. Kastrovna turned and saw the briefcase in the aisle. Crouching down, he saw Billy just three seats from the front.

"Get out of there, you dirty pig," Mr. Kastrovna shouted. "You set me up, you swine, and you're gonna pay dearly for it."

He grabbed Billy's collar and yanked him to his feet. Without hesitation he slammed the barrel of his gun across his face. Billy fell backwards toward a row of seats crying out in pain. As he slumped into the seat, blood streamed from his left cheek. He must have known that he was as good as dead.

The bodyguard apparently knew how to operate a bus as he shifted from one gear to another with relative ease. The coach rolled along at breakneck speeds, weaving in and out along the crowded roadway, occasionally clipping cars that were in the way. Heavy traffic, however, blocked the road ahead. The driver yanked the wheel hard to the right as the bus leaped over a curbstone and into a small park. I could see pedestrians running from the rolling monster. He turned the steering wheel quickly, and the bus again bounced over the sidewalk curbstone. Once back on the street, we crashed into two cars. They spun around, hitting a small truck and two other cars. The cluttered roadway instantly blocked all traffic. I saw drivers jump from their smashed vehicles screaming at the bus as it disappeared into the late-afternoon haze of exhaust. The road was blocked. The pursuing police could not get through. Our only hope of being saved now faded away. We were at the mercy of these killers.

Safely away from the police, the bus slowed to a normal speed and continued along Shadnevaza Boulevard, over a railroad crossing, and into a deserted warehouse. It pulled to a stop next to a black Mercedes sedan. Inside, a long flight of stairs led to a second floor platform and single doorway. Our noisy arrival alerted three men who emerged from the small room above. They watched as Mr. Kastrovna and his bodyguard dragged Billy from the bus below. I saw Billy stumble and fall twice as they pushed him up the rickety stairs. They soon disappeared into the room, slamming the door behind.

Erin and I shook with fear. We stayed huddled in the rear of the bus, praying that we wouldn't be discovered. We tried to develop a workable plan to free Billy. After about ten minutes we heard voices yelling something in Russian, and I raised my head just high enough to barely see out the side window.

"What's going on, Jimmy? I'm scared," Erin nervously whispered.

"I, uh, can see them dragging Billy down the stairs and into a corner near some metal barrels. Now they are tying him up in an old wooden chair. One of them just slapped Billy across the face," I told Erin.

Mr. Kastrovna yelled something at Billy as he held a pistol to his head. He then walked away to talk with the other four men who waited nearby.

"We gotta do somethin', Jimmy. We can't leave Billy there. They'll kill 'im."

"Yuh, I know. I'll think of somethin'."

I sat crouched on the bus floor with Erin, only occasionally raising my head to see what was happening outside. I had no idea what to do, yet Erin was counting on me for some kind of a plan.

"All the men are going back upstairs to that room again. Billy is still tied up in the chair. No one is guarding him. I think this is our best chance. What do you say, Erin?"

"Okay, Jimmy, let's untie him and we can all make a break for it. If we're quiet, they won't know we're gone until it's too late."

"Yuh, okay, let's go, but if they see us, I'll try to stop them somehow and you run like hell. Okay? Find some cops or get back to the hotel and tell Mr.

Reilly to send help," I said, hoping that our plan would work.

We quietly worked our way up the bus aisle and out the door that had been damaged earlier in a collision with one of the cars on the street. Using some stacked barrels for cover, we cautiously crept toward Billy. He looked up in surprise.

"Thank God," he whispered.

I quickly untied his hands and feet while Erin acted as a lookout.

"How'd you guys get here?" he asked.

"It's a long story, Billy. Tell you later. Let's not waste time now. We've gotta get out of here."

Just then the door to the office above opened and two men clomped down the wooden stairs toward us, and then stopped for a moment while one put a fresh magazine in his weapon and cocked it. They laughed as they headed towards Billy's empty chair. We stood there frozen, not knowing what to do. Their footsteps became louder and louder.

Chapter Thirteen

The Warehouse

Billy quietly picked up a large, heavy wrench that lay on a nearby table and pushed Erin and me behind the barrels. He followed us briefly, then stopped and slowly turned to confront whoever appeared. Almost immediately, the Russian yelled in disbelief that Billy was gone. He then ran back to alert Mr. Kastrovna and his bodyguard, who had already stepped out of the office onto the platform above. Billy raised his wrench and waited for the other henchman. The second gang member pulled out his gun and began searching near the stacked barrels and wooden crates that lined the outside walls. We could see his every movement between small openings. Soon he rounded the corner and stood just inches away from us. Billy swung the wrench downward, crashing into the man's skull. Slowly, the man slumped, unconscious, to the floor, landing with a loud thud, still tightly grasping his gun. Billy pried it loose from his clenched hand, shoved it under his belt, and signaled for us to follow him.

"I know what I'm doing," he said. "Trust me. I work for the Militia."

We were confused by his revelation and had no idea of what he was talking about, yet he seemed so confident and unafraid. He was certainly not the high school student we previously knew. We did as he ordered and hoped that all would turn out okay.

Almost immediately we heard sounds of the other thugs racing down the old wooden stairs yelling orders to their comrades. Mr. Kastrovna and his accomplice still remained on the upper landing observing the manhunt below. With drawn weapons, the gangsters searched for any signs of Billy.

Billy glanced back at Erin and myself and waved his hand as a signal for us to move further back into a small recess behind the old barrels lining the rear wall.

"Stay here. I'll be back," he whispered.

We had our doubts and prayed for his safety, as well as our own. We sat and waited, scared and nervous, Erin quietly began to cry. As I wiped away her tears, she threw her arms around me and held me tightly. I drew her close hoping to share what ever strength I still had left. I held her in my arms and thought back to happier and more secure times.

"Don't worry, Erin. We'll be alright. Billy knows what he's doing," I said bravely, while doubting my own convictions.

I was able to see through a small crevice between the tall stack of barrels. One of the gang was heading in Billy's direction. Billy also saw him and picked up something lying on the floor. He pitched it across the wide semi-darkened warehouse floor. It crashed into an empty barrel. The loud echoing sounds drew everyone's attention away from our location. Shots rang out as errant bullets echoed off the empty barrels. With everyone's attention now diverted, Billy was able to deliver another heavy blow, thereby knocking out the second thug. Billy appeared to have become both self confident and cocky as he continued to play his deadly game of elimination.

Creeping along the wall, Billy passed a fire alarm callbox. I saw him pull the greasy handle, setting off loud warning bells. Shots rang out as bullets ricocheted around him. One bullet punctured a barrel just in front of Billy. It immediately began spouting a small stream of liquid across the warehouse floor. Hope that's not gasoline, I thought. The bad guys certainly knew where the fire alarm callbox was located and continued to spray that area with automatic weapon fire. Ricocheting bullets bounced repeatedly among the metal barrels. The sounds of stray bullets echoed in our ears. I saw Billy crouch down out of the line of fire as slugs of hot metal whizzed by. Finally, a lull in the gunfire allowed him to take aim at another shadowy figure sneaking up on him. A short burst of gunfire spelled 'strike three' for the bad guys. One more to go, he thought, and then the big fish.

Mr. Kastrovna's bodyguard slowly climbed down the old wooden stairs and cautiously headed toward the wall where the fire alarm callbox was located. He spotted Billy and fired indiscriminately nearly hitting him. Billy was now barely two meters away from me.

The smell of gasoline fumes filled the air. The liquid was indeed a combustible fuel. Billy continued crawling along the wall, staying close to the floor. Inadvertently, he knocked over a barrel, and again, gunfire crashed into the walls and support columns around him. One bullet slammed into the growing puddles that now covered the floor. Sparks flared, igniting the gasoline with a loud swoosh and blinding light.

The brilliant glare and intense heat of the flames forced the fourth mobster away, yet he continued to fire his weapon blindly. Billy sent an empty barrel rolling his way, through the flames. It crashed into his legs as he fell backwards onto the flaming floor. He had been literally 'bowled over.' His cocked gun struck the floor first. A single gunshot rang out, followed by a scream of pain.

"Run, you guys," Billy screamed as the fire quickly consumed the old warehouse.

It seemed that Billy now had his sights set on Mr. Kastrovna himself. He could hear the wail of fire apparatus outside, along with the crackling and popping of the old wooden structure. Choking smoke filled the air, as we gasped and coughed.

Erin was frozen with fear and refused to leave the relative safety of the alcove where she hid, even though she choked on the noxious smoke. She began to cry loudly as I held her.

"Come on, Erin. We've gotta get outta here before we choke to death."

"I can't. I can't. They'll kill us," she cried.

"Come on. If we stay here we're as good as dead."

"Jimmy, don't leave me. I'm afraid," she sobbed.

"Don't worry. I won't, but let's get outta here now," I said, as I dragged her behind me.

She clutched my hand tightly, seeming to depend on me each step of the way, as we inched our way to the open doors just ahead.

The fire quickly climbed up the greasy walls igniting everything along its path. Tongues of flame were now lapping at the wooden stairs leading to the second floor. They, too, would soon be history, I thought. Through the smoke and haze, I saw Billy race up the wooden steps and onto the second floor landing waving his gun left and right, yet the elusive Mr. Kastrovna was apparently nowhere to be found.

Firemen battle warehouse inferno.

The ravenous flames and heavy black smoke nearly enveloped us as we stumbled along blindly. I pulled Erin, still crying, from the flaming inferno to safety outside just as one wall collapsed. The firemen were already spraying the doomed structure as we ran across the street, seeking the shelter of a fire truck. Several police vehicles had now arrived, and the police began to seal the area. We were still gasping for air to clear our lungs, as parts of the old building crumbled. I wanted to go back to help Billy, yet I didn't know what I could do. Besides, I knew Erin needed me with her.

Just then the black Mercedes screeched out of the burning inferno, driving over flaming debris and nearly hitting two firemen. Dropping their hoses, they dove from the path of the speeding sedan. With screeching tires, the car rounded the corner and disappeared.

Erin and I waited outside as Billy emerged, running from the burning building, yelling something in Russian to a nearby policeman. He then commandeered a police cruiser. Almost by instinct, I jumped in the back seat dragging Erin along with me. Billy screamed at us to get out.

"Not on your life," I yelled back. "We're into this too much to let you go it alone," I replied, without thinking it through.

Not wishing to waste another moment, Billy peeled off behind the fleeing Mercedes. Off we went, with sirens wailing and lights flashing. Mr. Kastrovna had a good lead on us. Billy tried to explain that this was the biggest drug operation ever in their department. He said that he had to have a good cover and that his department had conjured up the idea to pass him off as an American student.

He abruptly interrupted his story as the Mercedes turned down a small side street. We followed through the clouds of dust and exhaust that trailed behind it. We careened back out onto Pokov Boulevard and west past Cousew Avenue. Finally, the Mercedes turned right on Noskendrov Street. Mr. Kastrovna's car was easy to identify among all the old Skodas and Fiats that jockeyed for space with trucks, trams, and city busses. We had no difficulty following him.

Mr. Kastrovna's then swerved sharply onto Mindenkov Street at a very high speed. His two right wheels left the road, and the car flipped over, rolling side over side, and landing upright. Wheel covers flew off, spinning across the street. They crashed into trash barrels and parked vehicles. As we screeched to a halt next to his vehicle, Mr. Kastrovna jumped from the smoking wreck, ran to a nearby apartment building, scrambled up the stairs, disappearing inside.

Billy called for immediate backup on the police radio then told us to wait in the car for him. He took off after Mr. Kastrovna. Somewhat relieved and still mystified, we were all too happy to obey.

Erin regained some of her composure; nevertheless I could sense that this day was too much for her and that she wanted it to end. At the same time, I knew that our friendship had somehow turned to love. Oh, I don't mean passionate love, but a deeper love based on trust and mutual respect.

Later, I learned that Billy had located Mr. Kastrovna in someone's apartment. The mobster had burst in, taking an old retired man as hostage. Perhaps it was in an attempt to later work a deal for a possible escape to freedom. Billy said that he tried to talk Mr. Kastrovna into surrendering, while he impatiently waited for professional negotiators to arrive.

Indeed, additional police cars did arrive and sealed off the area. These uniformed police were trained in hostage negotiations and quickly took over the operation as Billy emerged from the building, exhausted and drained. He was still very concerned about the eventual outcome of the drama unfolding above him.

After nearly two hours of fruitless negotiating, a group of heavily armed men, maybe Moscow's version of a SWAT Team stood by for intervention. They seemed to hesitate, I imagined, because of the high probability that the hostage might be harmed. There was no progress, so they made plans to storm the building.

"What's your plan, chief?" Billy asked.

"If he doesn't come out, we're going in ten minutes," the chief responded.

"What about the people living in there? He might hurt them or use them as shields," Billy reminded him.

"We'll just have to be careful. Now, I'm busy so you'd better step aside," the chief ordered.

Billy backed off and told Erin and me about his conversation with the police chief. Television crews were now on the scene and had broadcast critical details of the police action. If the hostage had his television turned on, this information might have given Mr. Kastrovna a crucial edge. He could possibly swart any plans the police may have made. Meanwhile, the police continued their preparations to storm the building.

The minutes slowly ticked away. Finally, the chief waved the SWAT team on toward the building. They wasted no time, rushing the door, and disappearing up the inside stairwell. Billy remained at our side, yet remained focused on the operation.

After a long wait, the Captain finally bellowed something into his radio. Billy said that he wanted to know what was going on up there.

Over the static, we heard that they were in.

"There is an old man tied up to a chair but no one else," they reported.

Billy then relayed their response to us as we continued to wait.

"Mr. Kastrovna had disappeared yet again," Billy lamented.

Just then, I saw someone jump from the lower rungs of a fire escape on the side of the building.

"Hey, look," I screamed.

Billy and Erin also saw a man run toward the rear of the large complex. Billy took off after him through the tall, uncut grass, leaping over small toys left by careless children in their communal play areas. Erin and I followed as quickly as we could. When we reached the rear corner of the building, Mr. Kastrovna was already across the parking lot, attempting to climb a tall chain linked fence. Billy bolted after him, like a rabbit, across the parking area. Leaping up the fence, he managed to catch the old man's pants' legs before he dropped to the opposite side. Billy pulled him back, dragging him to the ground. They fought. At first I hesitated, and then I couldn't stand by any longer. I joined in to help Billy while Erin screamed for help. The police, hearing her screams, arrived and handcuffed Mr. Kastrovna.

Satisfied that Mr. Kastrovna had been finally arrested, we headed back toward the front of the apartment building. Then Billy suddenly stopped, turned, and returned to Mr. Kastrovna. He clenched his fist and punched the mobster squarely on the jaw, knocking him to the ground.

"That'll teach you not to pistol whip me, pal."

Billy stood there a moment, looking down at the cowering Mr. Kastrovna, and feeling quite macho. He was apparently satisfied that now another low-life would soon be off the streets.

"Come on, you guys. I think we both have a lot of explaining to do to each other. And what will Mr. Reilly have to say about your leisurely day of sightseeing in Moscow?" Billy smiled and asked.

Billy, Erin, and I chuckled and babbled on about each facet of this bizarre day. Strolling down the wide boulevard, filled with workers returning from their daily labors, we set out to find a good restaurant. We were starving!

Chapter Fourteen

Fancy Footwork

"Da Hotel Nazdanya has good restaurant. I think you like it. I pass for a good student. No? I think I had you fooled," Billy said, as we walked along the street.

"You did for a while," I said, "but I almost had you pegged. Your accent and ability to speak Russian without stumbling over words made me suspect that you weren't Danish, like you said you were."

"Yuh, I'm not Danish, but I do know some of da Danish words. I was afraid someone would ask me to speak da Danish and catch me," he continued.

"Well, just who are you anyway?" I asked.

"Oh, my name is Anatoly Pskov. Billy Martin is just made up name. I live here in Moscow so I know da city pretty well. Say, here is da Hotel Nazdanya that I tell you about. I know da hotel well. Eat here many times. Not expensive. We can all talk inside."

The red-bricked hotel was nestled between two commercial buildings and had been apparently renovated within the past year or two. Bright newly laid rugs sat on a polished granite floor. Judging by the doorman, it catered to an upper class cliental. Bellhops stood by, patiently awaiting the arrival of new guests. A pleasant desk clerk smiled as we passed through the lobby toward the inner restaurant.

Next to the reception desk was a bank of telephones. I decided it best to call Mr. Reilly back at the hotel. Luckily, I was able to get through and found him in his room. I told him much of what had happened earlier, although I omitted some of the scarier details. I could tell that Mr. Reilly was very upset about our getting involved with police work, and I knew we would have a lot more explaining to do after we got back to the hotel. That would have to wait, however, as the waiter was already taking Erin and Anatoly's orders.

As we ate, Anatoly explained that he worked for the Moscow Militia or police. He said that he was a rookie and had been kidded many times about his youthful appearance.

"Since I was da youngest member of da Militia and looked like a teenager, I was selected for da undercover work. I was assigned to your group with TAP's conditional approval. They didn't like any danger would come to da Americans, but I guess they didn't plan on you two," he laughed.

"Mr. Kastrovna's heroin operations were well known to police, but he had yet to be caught in an actual exchange," Anatoly continued. "Without proof, we couldn't build a good case against him. That's what we did today. We also get a couple other bad guys too."

Anatoly explained that he had been told that someone would make the initial contact with him at the hotel. That's where the peddler came in.

"My department had put da word out in the streets that an American with strong drug ties in the United States wanted to make a substantial 'buy' after he arrived in Moscow. We knew the word would find its way to Mr. Kastrovna, who was always hungry for a safe and easy sale," Anatoly explained. "I was then approached by the peddler outside the Metropole."

"Yuh, I saw that guy that met you. He was mixed in with those other peddlers near the bus the first morning we started our tour," I added.

"Yuh, that was him," Anatoly confirmed. "He was actually a well known informant. He said he would meet with the dealer, for a sum of money, and da dealer would arrange a meeting with the drug Overseer," Anatoly went on. "I gave the informant his payment at the circus and he provided me with an address where I would meet with the drug Overseer."

"This was at da apartment house where I met da drug Overseer and two of his goons. Da Overseer acted like a filter as well as an eliminator, if you know what I mean. Once I passed muster with each step in da ladder, a direct meeting with the Drug Lord would be set up. He didn't meet with just anyone, you know, but since I was buying about $500,000 worth of da white stuff, he agreed to meet me. This is why I visited the Militia this morning to pick up and sign for all that money. Yikes, the money!"

Anatoly jumped up, bolted to the phone, and frantically dialed. After several minutes he returned and told us that he was worried that the money might have burned up in the fire. He didn't know if the cash was still safely on the bus or if it and the bus both burned up back at that warehouse. Feeling quite relieved and more relaxed, he continued his story.

"They have da money and da dope as well. Thank God. Good firemen," he sighed. "I had to sign for da money, and if I lose it, I go to jail I think. Well, da money safe and Mr. Kastrovna sits in jailhouse. I think he will now be a guest at one of our fine Russian prisons for a long time to come."

Erin and I agreed. I thought that it would be best if we discussed all that happened today with Mr. Reilly without any further delay.

"We'd better get back to the hotel, Erin. Mr. Reilly is probably pretty darn mad at us and we'll be chewed out for sure. He's probably calling home right now and telling our parents everything. Are you ready?" I asked.

"Yuh, we'd better get goin'," she said while nodding in agreement.

She then implored Anatoly to come along with us.

"He'll never believe us, Anatoly. You must come and help us convince him that we are not making it all up," Erin pleaded.

Erin seemed to know that Mr. Reilly would be easier on us if Anatoly backed up our story.

"Yuh, Anatoly. You gotta help us," I repeated. "Bet he's already off the wall. We'll catch hell for sure if you don't come."

Although Anatoly had a long report to write, he finally agreed, and we all set off to the Hotel Metropole.

As expected, Mr. Reilly was waiting for us in the lobby. He looked stern and upset as we approached. He stared at us with his cold eyes. I knew he was furious that we had even got involved in Anatoly's undercover work. We never thought that we'd find ourselves in anything as strange and dangerous as we had today.

Jimmy and Erin face a cold reception.

"Where have you two been?" he demanded with a stern unforgiving expression. "You could have been killed."

His deep voice seemed to echo with a cold and heartless tone.

"We're sorry, but we were helping Billy, ah, I mean Anatoly," I nervously replied.

"Oh, so I see you know his real name too."

"Yuh, he told us when we stopped to get something to eat. That's when we called you on the phone." I replied.

Erin and I seemed to take turns explaining each detailed facet of today's unbelievably strange adventure. Anatoly corroborated our story.

"Oh, so that's how you got wrapped up with this. I see."

"Yuh, honest."

Mr. Reilly began to slowly lower his defenses and accept the story that we related. I was happy that Anatoly confirmed all that we said.

"Well, actually," Mr. Reilly explained, "I knew that Anatoly was an undercover agent for the Moscow Militia, but I couldn't let on to anyone. I had to keep it a secret. I was told about the plan by the TAP people when I called them from Stockholm. I reluctantly agreed with the TAP Program Director to assimilate Billy Martin, or should I say, Anatoly Pskov, into our delegation. It made it easier for him to pass himself off as an American student with stateside drug connections. This would be his cover and facilitate making the needed contacts," Mr. Reilly added.

"But wouldn't this be dangerous for the kids in our group," Erin inquired.

"Oh, I thought so, but I was assured that no student would be in any danger. All of Anatoly's dealings would be done away from the students, so I reluctantly agreed to let him join us. I objected naturally, but the TAP people said it was a done deal and requested that I cooperate. They also said that our State Department and the Russian's were involved and needed TAP as a cover. By the way, just how did you two initially get mixed up in this?" Mr. Reilly asked.

"I thought Anatoly was really a student, and I didn't want him to get into trouble. I saw him having secret meetings with strangers at all hours, so I told Erin. We decided to follow him today," I replied.

"Is that what really happened?" he asked, still somewhat skeptical.

Erin shook her head up and down in agreement.

"Yuh, honest. I didn't think anything bad was goin' to happen," I confessed. "We just wanted to keep Anatoly out of trouble. When I saw him getting involved with drug people, I tried to call you, but your cell phone doesn't work in Russia. I knew that Mrs. Kolinsky, Mrs. Renaud and you were out sightseeing, so I had no way to contact you or them all day."

"They were extremely helpful, Mr. Reilly," Anatoly said in support of us. "I want you to know that they saved my life today and should be commended not punished. I plan to talk about their bravery to my superiors tonight. They will be mentioned quite highly in my reports. Go easy on them," Anatoly begged.

"Well, okay. I've heard enough for one day. You two had better get some sleep. We will have a late sleep-in tomorrow and then leave for the airport after lunch. Thank you, Billy, ah, I mean, Anatoly for bringing them back safe and sound. How am I ever going to explain all this to their parents?" Mr. Reilly lamented.

Erin and I thanked Anatoly for everything and apologized for having him pegged wrong. We got his address and promised to write to him and then hurried off to our separate rooms while Mr. Reilly sat in the lobby a little longer talking with him.

Today's crazy adventure certainly seemed to be straight out of a Hollywood movie plot. How, I wondered, would I convince anyone of this unbelievable story. Mike was alone, lying on the bed when I entered our room. We chatted a while about his day's activities, and I briefly told him that Erin and I had wandered around some. I didn't want to get into details as he would hear the whole story tomorrow. Even though I was totally exhausted, I decided to scribble some of what happened in my journal. After a few paragraphs, I lay back on my bed, pulled the blankets up around my neck, and quickly drifted to sleep.

Chapter Fifteen

The Commissioner

Brrring! Brrring! The telephone sitting on the end table jangled continuously. Waving my arm in the general direction of the unrelenting ringing noise, I accidentally knocked the phone to the floor. From the dislodged receiver I could hear Erin's voice.

"Hello…hello. Jimmy, is that you?"

Still half asleep, I plopped my hand on the receiver and slowly dragged it to my ear.

"Yuh. Hi, Erin. What's up?" I said, rubbing my eyes and yawning.

"Mr. Reilly just called and wants both of us in the hotel dining room in thirty minutes. It's already ten o'clock and breakfast is over. Maybe he wants to chew us out for missing breakfast or maybe he wants to discuss details about our trip home. In any case, I don't think we should get on the wrong side of him today," she advised.

"Okay, I'm on my way. See you there," I said, as I hung up the phone and rolled out of bed.

Mike had left earlier, and apparently Erin and I slept later than the other members of our group. We later heard that Mr. Reilly had told Mike, my roommate, not to wake me when he got up for breakfast. Billy, or should I say, Anatoly, had returned to his own Moscow apartment the night before.

I quickly showered, shaved, and got dressed. After pulling some clean clothes from my suitcase, I threw my room keys into my pocket and ran down the empty hallway toward the elevator. I pushed the elevator button and smiled at the Floor Lady as I waited. She returned my smile and nodded as I dropped my key on her desk. The elevator finally arrived and the sliding doors slowly opened. To my surprise, Erin stood before me. She had taken the same elevator.

"Wow. Hi, Jimmy."

Then, without warning, she threw her arms around me and kissed me. Her soft, full lips met mine in a tender embrace. I could feel the warmth of her body pressed close to mine. I wrapped my arms around her and held her tightly. The Floor Lady looked up with a wide smile that brightened her face. Sudden outbursts of emotion were apparently seldom seen among the hotel guests.

"You were great yesterday, Jimmy, really great. I'm so proud of you and I hope you know that I like you a lot," she blurted.

"Oh, if you only knew just how scared I really was. I don't think I could go through another yesterday without you at my side. You gave me a lot of your strength too. I sure thought we'd be killed along with Anatoly."

"You did?"

"Yuh. When all that shooting was going on back at that warehouse, I thought they'd get Anatoly and then find us, and …"

"Shhh! I know, but let's not talk about it. I like you a lot, and don't want to think about losing you now or ever."

She then grasped my hand and held it tightly as the elevator slowly descended. There I was, completely caught off guard. Alone with Erin, feeling her love, and her sudden rush of pride which caused a lump to form in my throat. This was more than I could ever hope for. She stood proudly next to me as our elevator approached the lobby.

I finally gathered enough courage to tell her how I felt.

"Wow! You are really full of surprises, Erin. I hope you also know that I really, uh, like you too. Maybe we can go out together when we get back to the States. What do you say?"

"Of course, I was hoping we would," she replied. "I have to warn you that I won't let you get away that easily."

I now felt another rush of excitement and gently took her in my arms and returned her kiss, just as the elevator creaked to a stop at the lobby level and the doors opened widely.

"Ahem," said Mr. Reilly in a loud voice.

He stood outside the elevator's opened door apparently waiting for our arrival.

"What do you two think you're doing?" he asked. "Knock that stuff off. Don't you know that you're already in enough trouble and late for the meeting too? Better get into the dining room on the double and wipe that lipstick off your face, Jimmy."

"Yes sir," I said.

I was very nervous facing Mr. Reilly and started to tremble. His voice was stern and commanding. I was sure that he was still mad at us and would deal with us later. I felt embarrassed and somewhat scared that he would tell our parents. We both ran into the hotel dining room as fast as we could. As we raced through the doors, our whole delegation stood clapping and yelling 'Surprise.' Erin and I stopped cold. We were totally confused, and didn't know what was happening. Anatoly and three other official-looking men stood at the front of the dining room. Two really looked important and had many small medals pinned to their suit lapels.

We knew that we were in serious trouble when they called us to the front.

Anatoly came forward, kissed Erin on both cheeks and shook my hand. The three other men followed Anatoly's lead and also kissed Erin on both cheeks and shook my hand while the student delegation chatted continuously and snapped photos. We didn't have a clue as to what was happening.

Anatoly said that he had related all the events of yesterday to his superior. He said that his boss was so impressed with our bravery that he, in turn, called the Department Commissioner of the Militia to report the acts of bravery and courage that Erin and I showed in the capture of Mr. Kastrovna. The Department Commissioner said that he definitely wanted to meet these two brave Americans before they left Moscow. That is why we were all assembled this morning.

The Commissioner walked over to a small podium and spoke some words in Russian, which Anatoly translated into English. He told the students of all the events that had happened yesterday and then spoke about bravery, courage, and valor. He also explained that we proved to be exceptional ambassadors from the United States, and he was most honored to meet us and extend best wishes from the Republic of Russia. He went on thanking us for saving Anatoly's life and helping to apprehend a most dangerous drug kingpin, Mr. Kastrovna, and his network of gangsters. He said that our work helped foster better working relations between our two nations.

Erin and I stood there in a daze, caught completely by surprise, and rather embarrassed by this sudden, and unexpected, notoriety. After the speeches, the Department Commissioner pinned a shiny medal for 'High Bravery' on both Erin and me. It hung from a red ribbon. The Commissioner then kissed us on both cheeks and again congratulated us.

Mr. Reilly, who was never at a loss for words, seemed caught up in the emotion of the moment and gently wiped a tear from his eye. He then spoke about the worries that he and the other two chaperones had yesterday. I knew that he wasn't very happy with our wild escapades, but he said that once he knew the whole story, he felt very proud of the bravery and compassion we exhibited. He explained to the delegation that he had been informed by TAP headquarters, in Boston, that a young Russian policeman would join our group in Stockholm and that we should accept him as being just another American student.

"I was assured he could speak perfect English and easily blend into the American ways," Mr. Reilly explained. "I had no idea why he was joining the group except that he was in Special Operations and on a secret mission and that our group wouldn't be in any danger."

"This is one heck of a way to end a visit to Russia," I whispered to Erin. "I hope our next trip overseas won't be quite as exciting as this one. Just some boring city tours or visits to museums would suit me fine."

"Yuh, me too," Erin agreed.

She then turned to Mr. Reilly.

"Mr. Reilly, Jimmy and I had no idea what a wild adventure this would turn out to be. You should have seen how brave Jimmy really was. I'm so proud of him," she said while looking at me with obvious admiration.

The students who had listened so intently during this impromptu presentation now burst out laughing and clapping. We all laughed, relieving the tense seriousness of the moment. Mr. Reilly even gave us two thumbs up. Maybe he wasn't such an old fogy after all, I thought.

After we thanked the Russian dignitaries and gave a tearful farewell hug to our friend, Anatoly, we promised that we would write or e-mail him once we were back in the States. He also promised to answer our correspondence. Anatoly shook hands with Mr. Reilly and the other chaperones before leaving with his bosses.

Mr. Reilly reminded everyone to have their luggage in the lobby by twelve noon and to continue working on their journals. He said that today's events certainly called for a journal entry. This brought a chuckle to many. Erin and I laughed along with them.

He continued, "Lunch is set for twelve-thirty, and we'll leave at two o'clock for the airport. Don't be late."

Mrs. Kolinsky and Mrs. Renaud, who stood at the side of the large room, came over to offer their congratulations and almost immediately afterwards we were inundated by our friends who ran up to shake hands and look at the red ribbons and shiny medals that we proudly displayed on our shirts.

Slowly we made our way through the double doors and into the lobby.

"We'd better write all this down in our journal so we don't forget anything, Jimmy," Erin reminded me.

I turned to Erin, who again held my hand tightly, and said, "Yeah, you're right," and, with a broad smile, I continued, "You know, Erin, it doesn't get any better than this."

She winked at me and gave my hand a squeeze.

"You're right," she replied.

EPILOGUE

Unexpected Visitor

Ten years have now passed and I have just finished reading my old, Russian Teen Ambassador Journal for the 'umpteenth' time and reflected on the many events that connected Erin, Anatoly, Mike, and me so long ago. After all, it's been a long time since we were all in Russia, but I would never forget that week in Moscow. Earlier, I had pulled the old journal out from under a pile of old high school yearbooks to refresh my memory of my TAP days before our guest arrived.

Yes, I was commissioned as an Army Second Lieutenant, and traveled the world as I dreamed. Erin and I also became very close high school sweethearts and continued dating even through college and my Army years. She had majored in French and German and is now working as a middle school, foreign language teacher in Ostford, Massachusetts.

My two year stint with the Army eventually ended, and I returned home to settle down. Erin had written to me faithfully, and it was great to be back in her arms again. I soon joined an accounting firm in Boston, much to my father's disappointment. He had urged me to seek employment with his friend's New York financial management team. I seriously considered that golden opportunity, yet knew that such a distance would destroy my relationship with Erin. She had now grown into a stunning woman. She still had that attractive auburn hair and shy demeanor. I always knew that she would be the girl for me.

Before long, Erin and I tied the knot and we are now happily married with a handsome baby boy of our own. Yup, we named him Billy, in honor of Anatoly Pskov's undercover alias. After all, it was Anatoly who really brought us together and cemented our relationship.

We corresponded with Anatoly for a couple of years after our trip to Moscow and learned that he had been promoted to Senior Station Chief in the Special Operations Department. He still liked his unpredictable assignments. Maybe one day we will again see Anatoly if we ever re-visit Moscow.

After our old, teen ambassador days back in 1994, we became good friends with Mike Stevens. He always remembered our harrowing escapades in Moscow and how the story of our adventure made front-page headlines in all the local papers, and even ran in the Boston Tribune.

Earlier in the week, he called to say that he would be in Boston on business and wanted to stop by to see us. We hadn't seen him in years and were most eager to have him visit. Naturally we invited him to dinner, as this was certainly a reunion we didn't want to miss.

A sudden knock on the door broke my trance. I threw my journal aside and raced to greet our impatiently awaited visitor.

I had lost touch with Mike soon after graduation from college when I went on active duty with the Army, and he attended some graduate school in Ohio. Now, here he was and there was much more catching up to do.

"Hey, Erin, he's here," I yelled.

She had just finished setting the table and scurried to the door just behind me. Opening the door, we looked in amazement at the visitors standing before us. There were Mike and Anatoly.

"Hope you don't mind if I brought a friend," Mike said with a smile. "I thought that you might remember him."

"Remember him? Of course, we do," I yelled in disbelief.

Erin covered her mouth as tears quickly swelled in her eyes, then slowly slipped down her cheeks as she and I gave both of them bear hugs and shook their hands vigorously.

"Come in, come in," we pleaded.

Anatoly and Mike made themselves comfortable in the living room and chatted about their lives while we filled them in on our exploits and introduced them to little Billy who was fast asleep in the nursery. Anatoly was shocked and honored that we would name our first born after him.

"What? You name your boy after me?" he said in disbelief. "I don't believe it. I am most honored."

"If it wasn't for you, Anatoly, Erin and I wouldn't have been drawn so close. We have you to thank."

"Yuh, maybe it takes some good action and excitement like we both shared back in Moscow, don't you think?" he laughed.

Anatoly then changed the subject and told us about his new two bedroom apartment in Moscow and his many responsibilities with the Special Operations section. He said he was now in training for a newly organized Joint Operations Department that required working with foreign police agencies. With his excellent English speaking ability, he was selected to attend a two-month training program with the New York State Police. Anatoly said that he also was now married and had two small children of his own. His wife worked as an administrative assistant in some governmental agency.

Mike then filled us in on his news. He said that he had landed a great job as an oil company representative for Arcon Oil. Although still single, he told us that he was quite happy with his life and job, even if it did involve much travel. Apparently, with all his traveling, he never found time to establish any kind of long term relationship. He and Anatoly had stayed in contact with each other over the years and had jointly planned this surprise ten-year reunion. Boy, we were certainly surprised, all right.

After dinner we retired to the den. As Erin poured coffee, Anatoly asked about our days following the Moscow incident.

"We certainly were famous for awhile," I said. "We were interviewed on television and also had our stories in all the papers. Actually, I rather enjoyed it."

Erin had just placed a tray of desserts on the coffee table and looked at me with an inquisitive expression.

"What?" she inquired. "You actually liked all those people questioning our every move and then telling the world?"

"Yuh. Can't say that we weren't well known," I said while winking at Erin.

Erin slowly shook her head in disagreement, but said nothing further.

Mike and Anatoly smiled as they had caught me winking at Erin.

"It was the same in my country," Anatoly acknowledged. "No rest from everyone asking questions, questions, and more questions. I was so happy when other news took center attention."

"What ever happened to Mr. Kastrovna, Anatoly?" I inquired.

"Oh, he was tried not only for drugs but also murder. His case came up three months after you left. It was then delayed for another three months so that the lawyers had more time to prepare. When it was all over, he received thirty years to life in our fine prisons. One of his bodyguards also recovered from the gunshot wounds and was sentenced to ten years."

"I guess everything turned out as it should. I don't have any desire, however, to relive that crazy week again. Before you two arrived, I had been reading my old journal and again realized that we had some really scary moments back in '94," I added.

"It's a different country today," Anatoly said. "There are many new buildings there, and even the old Metropole has had a facelift. Maybe you should all visit Moscow again to see the changes that have taken place. You would not believe it."

"Oh, I couldn't leave the baby," Erin joined in. "Such a long trip would be too hard on him."

"Well," Anatoly continued, "maybe Mike and Jimmy could return to Moscow with me. I could really show them the city. They could all stay at my apartment too."

That sounds great," Mike said. "I am long overdue for some vacation time. Count me in. What do you say, Jimmy?"

"Hmmm," I thought.

Erin's mouth dropped as she held her breath. She raised her eyebrows and stared at me, awaiting my reply. It seemed to be my decision and I thought about it a long time. The stillness within the room was broken only by the ticking clock on the wall. Mike and Anatoly looked at each other quietly and waited for my decision.

This seemed like a great opportunity and I did have vacation time coming. After all, I hadn't seen these guys in a long time. Erin would hopefully understand. On the other hand, she was the light of my life and I cherished every moment that we shared together. To leave her would bring only heartache and loneliness to both of us. After a long, long pause, I finally replied.

"Guess not this time, guys. I've got a baby to think of, and Erin and I are just fine right here. Maybe next year."

We all laughed as she threw her arms around me and kissed me on the cheek. She then turned to our guests, breathed a sigh of relief, and said "Yuh, maybe next year."

Agreeing to keep in touch, we reminisced until nearly midnight. After their departure, Erin and I sat on the couch and chattered about such an unexpected and successful reunion.

Erin, nearly exhausted, snuggled up to me and asked, "Honey, would you really go to Moscow without me?"

I hesitated a long while before replying, "Hmmm."